Amish 1

MW01087311

Book 1

RUTH PRICE

Published by Global Grafx Press, LLC. © 2013

The Pennsylvania Dutch used in this manuscript is taken from the Revised Pennsylvania German Dictionary: English to Pennsylvania Dutch (1991) by C. Richard Beam, Brookshire Publications, Inc. Lancaster, PA 17603

The Bible quotations used in this manuscript are taken from the King James Bible.

ISBN-13: 978-1508691716
ISBN 10: 1508691711

CONTENTS

Even in laughter the heart is sorrowful; and the end of that mirth is heaviness.

– Proverbs 14:13

CHAPTER 1

As the car pulled down the driveway towards the squat, white farmhouse between the family cornfield and chicken coop, Sarah Lambright was filled with both longing and fear. Her Rumspringa was over. Though she'd loved the energetic hum of New York City and the harsh vibrancy of the Arizona deserts when she'd traveled with Englischer friends across country last summer, she wasn't suited to Englischer life. The music was too charged, the conversations too trivial, and people fell in and out of love as though the emotion was a set of cheap shoes that fell apart between one season and the next.

No, Sarah's best memories of the past two years had been apprenticing to teach with her aunt in Ephrata. The connections she'd made to her young scholars, the joy of knowledge kindled in their bright gazes, playing softball with them after lunch, this was her place, and her soul vibrated with the hope that she'd soon have her own schoolhouse, her own students, and with God's help, her own husband and home.

"You're here, young lady," the driver said, slowing into the groove behind the family buggy. She was an older woman with ropes of black hair salted with gray and pulled back beneath a bright yellow scarf that matched the daisies on her blouse.

"Danki," Sarah said, falling instinctively into the language of her childhood. "Thank you." It occurred to her that she didn't know the older woman's name, and Sarah felt briefly ashamed. She'd been so pensive during the ride. Though she'd come home for Second Christmas and once for a week last summer, she'd been a visitor then. Now, just as the light green stalks of corn reached once again for the sun, her life was also starting anew. She only prayed that the District elders would accept her as a suitable replacement for Mrs. Troyer, who was leaving her post after six years to get married and have her first child.

From the fields, one of her brothers, Samuel by the size, waved vigorously and began to run to the car, Bandit, the family mutt, dogging his heels. He shouted something. Sarah couldn't hear it over the car's air-conditioning, but the cornstalks behind him shook as she glimpsed her daed and youngest brother stepping from the corn. This time of morning, mamm was probably in the garden behind the house, tending to her plants. Then Sarah caught a whiff of cinnamon and her heart leapt. Friendship Bread! Her mamm must have made a batch!

The driver reached into her glove compartment and handed Sarah a business card. "My name's Elsie," she said. "If you're in need of a driver again."

"Sarah." They shook hands.

Elsie said, "Let me help you with those bags."

"Nee," Sarah waved the offer aside. "My brothers and I can handle it." Her four younger brothers had handled much in Sarah's absence, all complaining that they'd had to take their turns helping mamm with the cooking and washing though that was women's work.

At that moment, Sam skirted in front of the car to Sarah's door and pulled at the handle. Bandit jumped up behind him, barking furiously. They'd found him as a puppy by the side of the road coming home from church five years back. He was a Jack Russell mix, white and tan with a splotch of brown over his right eye (earning him his name) and a matching one on his rump.

"One second," Elsie said, tapping the automatic lock. Sam pulled again, and stumbled back as the door pulled free.

Sarah laughed. "Sam," she said, stepping out of the car. Bandit immediately jumped up on her leg, his paws resting just below her knee. Sarah leaned down to rub his head. "Danki."

"You're laughing at me," Sam said, wrinkling his nose. Unlike the rest of the kinner, whose hair had darkened to auburn or brown by age eight or nine, Sam had kept the blond of his childhood, and it shone in messy curls beneath his straw hat. He'd be twelve in November, and he drew himself up to his full eleven and three-quarter years of gravitas as he said, "Judgments are prepared for scorners, and stripes for the back of fools."

Sarah's grin widened. "You've been studying!"

"We still have to memorize a verse a day and talk about it over dinner."

"I missed that," Sarah said. Though she'd kept up with her Bible, of course, but it wasn't the same.

"You would," Sam said, but he was grinning. "Where's your stuff? How long are you staying this time?"

"Until I'm married," Sarah said.

Sam rocked back on his feet. "You're really staying!" he shouted, throwing his arms around her waist and squeezing tightly enough to hurt. "Wunderbar!"

"Not so tight!" Sarah coughed, but hugged her brother back. Her eyes were wet. Ridiculous to start crying now. She'd seen them all less than five months ago.

"Sarah, it's a blessed day." A large hand rested on her shoulder as her daed said in his deep baritone. "I hadn't known you were coming so early."

Sam looked up, loosening his grip at last. "Daed, Sarah's going to take her vows!"

"Is this true, Sarah?" Her daed asked.

"Ja," Sarah turned to face him.

"Gutt!" He swallowed, and then took a breath, his expression one of profound joy. "I am so proud of you. Aren't we proud?" He glanced at his two other sons, Atlee and Willis, on either side him.

They nodded. Atlee, the youngest, was a round-faced six-year-old with bright blue eyes and full, curling lashes that Englischer girls used all manner of cruel looking instruments to fabricate. He held a leaf between his pudgy fingers, his attention caught between twirling it in the sunlight and brief glances at his newly returned sister. Willis, at least, seemed interested in Sarah. He hooked his thumbs in the waistline of his trousers as he stared up at her.

"We'll need to get my bags out of the car," Sarah said. "I'm sure Elsie has other clients."

Elsie laughed from inside the car. "Take your time, child. I haven't got anyone else to pick up until three this afternoon, and that's just taking Mrs. Watlington to the store."

"Sam, Willis, go get Sarah's bags," Sarah's daed ordered. "Atlee, your mamm must be in the coop with those chickens.

She'd be blessed to hear anything over their squawking." He was diplomatic enough not to say that her mamm was in the habit of taking out her hearing aid when doing simple work around the house, "And we weren't expecting you until after lunch, but she'll never forgive us if we let her miss her daughter's homecoming."

"Ja," Atlee said, and dropping the leaf, took off running towards the chicken coop.

"We'll speak with the Bishop at church this Sunday," her daed declared. "Step over here, Sarah, into the light."

Sarah did so, and he smiled. "You've become a fine woman, Sarah. A fine woman."

And with that, Sarah was folded into the loving arms of her family.

CHAPTER 2

Since their mamm had been taken away at the end of March, Fannie Graber's home had fallen into silence. Even Rachel, the youngest of the kinner at six-years-old, played silently with her dolls and jammed her thumb into her mouth, sucking on it as though to swallow her own words. Their family was the surface of a dark pond, everyone doing their duty as they ought with neither laughter nor affection. Waneta, the oldest, took over the household chores with the help of her younger sisters: cooking, cleaning and taking care of the kinner. Their daed worked at the factory and then came home to tend the fields, as always.

Fannie worried about her family, but couldn't find the courage to challenge the silence. At night, she prayed, tears soaking into her pillow, that as their grief eased, the weight of it would ease as well and they'd come together again.

Sometimes, when Fannie drifted off, she imagined phantom fingers in her hair and a warm, comforting voice, "Take care, child, this too shall pass." But these dreams were meaningless in the harsh light of dawn.

Nobody told Fannie what was wrong with their mamm and why

was it taking so long for the doctors to help her. The longest she'd been gone before was two weeks, but now it had been almost five. Only Fannie's daed knew why, and he kept the knowledge locked like treasure behind his teeth.

"When she's better, she'll come back," was all her daed said on the subject. "Until then, we keep your mamm in our prayers."

All of this, Fannie could endure. She had a talent for enduring. She put up with her older sister Waneta's bossiness and the afternoons she'd barricade herself in her parents' empty bedroom room, sometimes for hours, leaving Fannie to take on all of the housework. She endured her younger brother Abel's kicking at her calves, and her youngest sister Rachel pulling at her ears and kapp strings. Fannie had endured her mamm's slow change from warm hugs, easy smiles and happiness to her flashes of fury and drawing in on herself as though the very light was attacking her and whispering accusations that she said stabbed like the nails of crucifixion in her eyes.

As April warmed and brightened into May, their daed seemed farther removed than ever. Sometimes Fannie would overhear him and Waneta arguing in harsh whispers behind the barn, but when they saw Fannie both would fall back into silence.

In May, after a youth soccer game, Waneta began to smile again.

"Did you meet someone?" Fannie asked, after the second day of her sister humming cheerfully, albeit off-key, over the dishes.

"Meet...no..." Waneta said, with a mysterious smile. "But Jebediah was there."

"Isn't he traveling across the country with some Englischer friends?"

"He was, and I thought he might not return home, but he remembers our promise."

"Promise?"

Waneta's smile widened, her arms elbow deep in sudsy water. "When we were children, we promised we'd court with each other and get married. He chose me specifically for his team on Saturday, and we spoke at the Fellowship afterwards. Of course, we all had to stay with the group under the eye of Mrs. Troyer, but as a woman, you can tell when a man is interested. That's what mamm says. He'll be making his wishes known shortly."

Fannie was thrilled to see the light rekindled in her sister's eyes, but she couldn't help but wonder, if Jeb were interested in Waneta, wouldn't he have done something by now? Even if he were too traditional to speak with her daed before the wedding announcement, he certainly would have made an opportunity to see Waneta in secret, and Fannie would have known. "It's been over a week," Fannie ventured. "He hasn't visited at all?"

"He will," Waneta said. "He has to."

Frightened by the fervor of her sister's expression, Fannie nodded. "Okay."

"You're too young to look so serious!" Waneta said and before Fannie knew what happened, flicked a clump of soap fluff at her forehead.

"Hey!" Fannie shouted and ducking under her sister's arm grabbed a handful of soap and smeared it across her sister's chin. Soon they were laughing together, soap suds falling like snow on the floor.

Rachel, who had fallen asleep, her head cradled in her left arm on the kitchen table, looked up. Pulling her thumb from her mouth, she asked, "What's funny?"

The two older girls' gazes met. "Get her," Waneta said. Within minutes, the kitchen was a mess of soap and laughter. At that moment, Fannie vowed she would do whatever it took to keep that light in her older sister's eyes. When their mamm came back, their family would be whole and happy. By God.

CHAPTER 3

They had Church at the Lapp's, a family on the east side of the district, far enough away that even getting up early for the morning chores and with Sarah's extra set of hands besides, they still didn't arrive until well after the church buggy had been unloaded. Most of the other parishioners had already parked, watered their horses and let them out to graze in the pasture. As her daed drove to the end of the line of buggies, two boys ran out to meet them.

"We'll take your horse, sir," the taller one said in Pennsylvania Dutch. His face was red and dusted with acne across the forehead. He smiled brightly, the grin given character by a chip in his left, front tooth. "Service will be starting in about fifteen minutes.

"Danki," her daed said, handing the reins over. "Keep clear of her left flank. Sandy likes to kick."

Before her Rumspringa, Sarah hadn't been so aware of the sound of her own language. Even in Ephrata, the accent had been a bit harsher, the men especially pushing their ch's to the back of their throat when excited. These tiny differences made Sarah's homecoming clear to her.

The day was overcast. A group of teens milled near the entrance of the barn. At this distance, with their plain clothes and hair demurely tucked under their bonnets, Sarah couldn't discern her friends Ruth and Hannah from the group. The only one she recognized for sure was Fannie, who stood a head taller than the other girls and had developed a slight stoop to her shoulders to compensate for her extra height. She was only fifteen, and in spite of her height had always stood in the shadow of her older sister Waneta, who was a year older than Sarah and had always kept to herself, never seeming close to the girls her own age.

"We'll need to see these plates to Mrs. Lapp before you run off to see your friends," Sarah's mamm said to the four of them as Sarah's daed stepped down from the front of the buggy to help the other two boys. "Abel's wife is having trouble so late in her term, so I don't know if your brother will be here," she added to Sarah, handing her a full glass serving pan of potato salad.

Sarah nodded, unsurprised. Her brother's wife, Katie, was a frail woman: pale skinned with corn silk hair and light blue eyes that reminded Sarah of a soap bubble. Abel had met Katie at an inter-district sing four years back, and they'd fallen almost instantly in love. Abel wouldn't be likely to leave her side until the baby was born, and both mother and child were safe.

Sarah held the serving plate carefully in the crook of her right arm as she climbed down from the buggy. On her way to the house, she caught sight of her friend Annie. Sarah's friend had lost the chubbiness of her youth, the hourglass of her figure apparent even through her simple navy dress and white apron. Even so, her brown curls still had a flyaway nature that refused to be tamed by comb or prayer kapp.

Sarah waved with her free and hand shouted, "Annie!"

"Sarah!" Annie rocked forward on her toes. She whirled around and waved the other girl to her. "Ruth, it's Sarah! Come on." Not waiting to see if Ruth had heard her, Annie jogged across the driveway towards Sarah. "I'm so glad you're back! And what's that?" she asked, pointing at the loaf pans that Sarah was carrying. "Did your mamm make her Friendship Bread? I know it all starts out the same, but your mamm does something with hers that's just perfect. Has she given you her recipe?"

"Nee," Sarah said. "Not until I'm baptized, she said."

"You're going to take your vows though, right?"

"Ja," Sarah said, grinning. "I want to be a teacher."

"I knew it. Mrs. Troyer will be stepping down in the fall. Is that why you came back?"

"Ja, at least in part. I also missed being home," Sarah said. "Walk with me. I have to put these in Mrs. Lapp's kitchen for the fellowship."

"Ja, ja."

Annie linked Sarah's free arm in hers. From behind Sarah came the sound of running footsteps. "Sarah!" It was Ruth. "I'm sorry, my sister wouldn't let me go. She's got a crush on John. Just like all of the girls her age. If I were a bit younger even, but….I wiped his nose all winter when he was in first grade."

Sarah started laughing. "Johnny-snotface!" The nickname sprang from Sarah's lips immediately, though, upon saying it, she felt a stab of guilt. As a teacher, she shouldn't support name calling, not that he'd hear or even care at this point.

"I know. I know," Ruth said. She was taller than both Annie and Sarah, willowy with long black hair dark and shiny as an inkwell. Of the three of them, Ruth had been most likely to leave and pursue an Englischer life. The other girl still might decide to do so, but Sarah was grateful that her friend was with her now. Ruth asked, "So you're going to be teaching then?"

Sarah nodded for a third time.

"Well, you'll need a husband then," Ruth said, ever practical. "Right now, we've three boys from other districts apprenticing here, Jacob, Isaac, and Abram. Annie's sweet on Mark, and, of course, there's the boys from school, Daniel, Amos, Zachariah, and Jeb. Jeb's just gotten back from an apprenticeship, like you except in furniture making, and he traveled with Zach to the West Coast with some Englischers."

"Dear Heavens, Ruth," Annie cut in. "Sarah hasn't even been back for services in two years. Give poor her a moment to breathe."

Sarah laughed, glad for the warmth of her friends. Of course, she had also made friends in Ephrata, but none could be as close as her school chums, and she enjoyed their news. Would she be interested in a local boy? As much as she loved her life here and teaching, she didn't want to do it alone. God would see to it that the right man was put into her path. She just needed to have faith.

They walked up the steps to the porch of the Lapp's farmhouse. It was small for an Amish residence, and though they'd painted it white in the Amish style, the house itself still had an Englischer feel to its design, which made sense considering the Lapps bought their farm from an Englischer family five years ago. Ruth pushed the door open.

"Mrs. Lapp," she called out, walking down the hallway to the back of the house. The farmhouse, the skylights of an Amish residence, shrouding the hall in a murky darkness, but when they turned into the kitchen, two wide bay windows let in the sunlight, lending the small room a homey cheer. Mrs. Lapp at on a stool by the oven. She was only six years older than Sarah, with three kinner, the baby boy gurgling in the bassinet beside her and a pair of fraternal twins now age three that she'd had to give birth to in an

Englischer hospital for safety's sake.

Mrs. Lapp looked up as they entered and said, "Just put that in the refrigerator. Danki." The young woman looked exhausted, her skin an unhealthy pale and dark circles under her eyes.

"Are you okay?" Sarah asked.

"Ja," the woman said. "I'm fine. I was just staying here for some quiet. The baby kept me up half of the night. He's like a cat, screams all night and then sleeps half of the day, heaven help me."

"If there's anything you need..." Sarah started, and Annie echoed, "Ja, we don't live so far from here. Only twenty minutes by buggy. My mamm and I will bring by some of our extra baking on Tuesday. She's still cooking for eight of us even though my two brothers and our sister have gotten married and set up their own households, so it's really no trouble."

"I couldn't," Mrs. Lapp said, but she looked relieved when Annie insisted.

"It's really no trouble," Annie said, taking Mrs. Lapp's hands. "You'll be doing us a favor. I'm feeling stuffed to my ears with bread and sweets."

"Danki," Mrs. Lapp said, her shoulders relaxing. "You girls should get to church. We'll be along shortly. It's good to see you back, Sarah," she added.

They returned to the barn just as people began filing in. The oldest men entered first with the Bishop, following them on the opposite side of the aisle, the married and baptized women with their babies and toddlers, following them the unbaptized teens and youths. As Sarah walked in with the young women, her gaze locked with a young man. At first she thought him a stranger, one of the men apprenticing from a different district, but there was something familiar in his open, expressive face that made Sarah question her first assumption. She liked his face. His eyes were set a bit wide, large and bright amber that caught the light like fresh honey.

When the young man smiled, the familiar set of his features became recognizable. Her cheeks warmed as she smiled back.

"Is that Jeb?" Sarah whispered to Annie.

Annie nodded. "I didn't believe it either! He used to be such a stick."

Then the men and women parted, women moving to seat themselves on the benches on the left side of the barn while the men sat on the right. Sarah wanted to catch his gaze again, and she looked over the young men, trying not to be too obvious in her curiosity. Was this man really same boy she'd caught fireflies with as a girl? She remembered him as almost skeletally thin, scarecrow of bones that seemed far too large for his skin.

When they took their places on their bench towards the back wall of the barn, Annie leaned in and whispered, "Be careful though, I think Waneta's got her eye on him. She's cornered him after the last volleyball game."

"So they're courting then?" Sarah ventured, quashing the stab of regret that accompanied that thought.

The Bishop stood. "Let's begin," he said.

As Mr. Lapp hummed the first note of the Loblied, the hymn of praise that began every church service, Annie shook her head.

So Jeb wasn't courting Waneta! It shouldn't have made Sarah so excited, but in spite of her best efforts to focus her attention on the prayers and praise of the Lord, Sarah's thoughts wandered back to Jeb through the service. She'd always liked him. Unlike Zachariah, who had put worms in her lunchbox once, Jeb had been kind. She hoped he would speak with her after the service.

A bit of the Bishop's talk managed to distract Sarah from her reverie. "Psalm 37:4. Delight thyself also in the Lord: and he shall give thee the desires of thine heart."

Just that, Sarah prayed. *Amen.*

CHAPTER 4

The weather was warm enough that the Fellowship luncheon was held outside. Long tables were brought out from the home and Church buggy and organized in rows in the open space between the house and barn. Sarah joined the other women in bringing out plates of food, pitchers of iced tea and hot coffee, plates, bowls and silver.

Normally the married men ate first, the oldest having first choice of the food, but the picnic gave enough room for everyone to eat at once. Sarah helped with serving the drinks, a madcap of activity until the married women shooed Sarah and her friends away. "Eat! Eat!"

Sarah gratefully took her plate and spooned it high with delicacies of home, corn and potato salad, warm, dense breads, oven fried chicken, macaroni salad, onion cake and cool, tart lemonade. Most of the young women took their plates and seated themselves on a warm patch of grass near the garden. They sat in a rough circle atop a large cloth, with Sarah between Ruth and Annie and Waneta and her younger sister Fannie across from them. Waneta seemed more annoyed than anything as she speared at her string bean casserole.

"I was worried in might rain," Ruth said. "Looking at the sky this morning. I'm glad it didn't."

"Me too," Sarah agreed.

The sound of laughter and stomping boots made Sarah raise her gaze from her food. Waneta looked up, as well. "There's Zach and Jeb," she said, the annoyance wiped from her brow and replaced by a too-bright smile as she waved at the boys. "Jebediah," she shouted, waving the two young men over.

Amish custom forbade unmarried men and women to spend time alone together, but such strictures were relaxed for unbaptized youths, the purpose of their Rumspringa in large part to find a partner to love and marry.

Zach and Jeb crossed over to the girls. "Wie Geht's?" Zach said with an easy grin, asking how they were.

Sarah joined the others in a chorus of "gutt." Her gaze flitted to Jeb, trying to maintain some semblance of propriety in spite of her roiling emotions. She wished for a moment for the easy ways Englischers had between men and women, but at the same time she doubted she'd have the bravery to speak with him directly and alone. An exchange of smiles might simply be an expression of friendship. He hadn't seen her in years, so maybe the strength of his gaze was more curiosity than interest. She couldn't presume.

Zach chattered on a bit about a movie he'd seen at the Englischer theater last night, something with robots.

"Aren't those mechanical people?" Fannie asked. "Do the Englischers really use them in their homes to clean?"

"Not seriously," Zach said. "Isn't that right Jeb?"

"I never saw one," Jeb said. "But not all of us here are on our Rumspringa, so it's probably better not to talk about this now."

"I'll be sixteen in October," Fannie said, indignantly.

"Will you two be staying for the Sing on tonight?" Waneta asked. Though the question was directed at both boys, her gaze remained fixed on Jebediah, who seemed not to notice or at least not return the attention. Sarah's heart brightened.

Sarah desperately wanted to, but with the Lapps living on the opposite side of the district and her mamm and the kinner needing to be in bed at a decent hour, she wasn't sure how it would be possible for her to stay so late. As the other youths chimed agreement, Sarah found herself shaking her head. "I don't think...not today."

Annie took her hand. "Oh, but you just got back!" she exclaimed.

"I can't justify having my family stay late," Sarah said.

"You can ride with us," Jeb said. "My farm is just a mile and a half from yours, and I'll be riding with Deacon Yoder in the church buggy."

"Are you sure?" Sarah asked, joyfully. With the Deacon in the buggy, there could be no insinuation of impropriety. At the same time, she'd be able to stay for the sing and have some time to speak with Jebediah. It also warmed Sarah immensely that he had suggested driving her so freely.

"It's no trouble," Jeb said with a shy smile. The young men stayed a bit longer before someone else called them away. When they left, Annie turned to Sarah and said in a teasing tone, "Jebediah was very kind to offer you a ride home."

"Ja," Sarah said, and took a large bite of her potato salad in an effort to keep from embarrassing herself by saying something foolish.

"Jebediah is kind," Waneta cut in, her tone acid. Her younger sister Fannie stared wide-eyed, her gaze flitting between the two older girls. As always, Fannie sat slightly hunched as though striving constantly to make herself smaller.

Jumping to Sarah's defense, Ruth said, "I think he likes her."

"He was only being kind to an old friend," Waneta said with an air of finality. "Come on, Fannie. We were supposed to be helping Mrs. Lapp in the kitchen."

Fannie looked down at her plate. She had only eaten half of her food, but she picked it up and jumped to her feet. "Ja!" she said, nodding her head a bit too vigorously. "We did say we'd help with the baby."

"Exactly right."

When the two girls had gone, Ruth turned to Sarah and said, "We're all supposed to be forgiving of Waneta, what with her mamm."

"Her mamm?" Sarah had heard nothing of Waneta's family while in Ephrata. "Is she ill again?" Waneta's mamm had been prone to sickness; Sarah remembered from school. Because of this, her family never hosted church.

"Something like that," Ruth said, at the same time Annie said, "I heard she's gone crazy."

"What?"

Ruth reached across Sarah and smacked Annie on the arm. "It's a sin to spread gossip."

"My mamm and aunt were talking about it last week over the baking," Annie said. "And my mamm doesn't gossip. They were just discussing if they'd need to send over extra cooking and help with the wash since her mamm had been sent to Philhaven, but it seems Waneta and Fannie have it in hand."

Sympathy filled Sarah. She couldn't imagine how difficult it would be if her mamm were not the rock of her home, having instead suffered a break in her mind or heart. Though most of her education in teaching had come through apprenticeship as was the Amish way, she had taken some classes at the local community college, including an introduction to Psychology. She'd found herself enraptured at the varying theories Englischers used to understand the mind, and while she found some of it overly complex, it gave her a firm appreciation for how a person could suffer if they had some sort of mental ailment. Maybe that was why Waneta had always been so prickly. If she'd had to deal with so much turmoil in her home, it would make her lash out at the world.

"It still must be difficult," Sarah said.

"Still, you'll want to be careful. It looks like she's set her sights on Jebediah, and she won't be much pleased if he doesn't return her affections."

Sarah shrugged. "I don't think it will be much of a problem. Waneta will find someone else. She certainly isn't going to want someone who isn't interested in her."

Ruth nodded, but Annie's expression remained dubious.

"My daed said he'd arrange for me to speak with the Bishop so that I could talk with the District elders about starting to teach in the fall," Sarah said, wanting to change the subject.

"That's great," Ruth chimed in. "Do you think you'll need to speak with him today?"

"I should at least give my regards," Sarah said. She picked up her plate, stood, and shook the grass from her dress. "Let me just return this to the kitchen. We should also check to see if we can help Mrs. Lapp with anything," she added. "The poor woman really does look exhausted."

"You're right," Annie said, smiling and, walking in step, the three girls carried their plates back towards the house. Even so, Waneta's anger hung like a black mist over Sarah's thoughts, and she couldn't forget Annie's earlier statement that something was truly wrong, something that could lead the troubled girl to make a terrible, irrevocable mistake.

CHAPTER 5

Jebediah Stoltzfus walked with best friend Zachariah around the back of the barn to join with the other young men.

"I said Sarah liked you," Zach said, laughing as he popped a piece of fried chicken into his mouth. "And Sarah sure has gotten pretty since she went to Ephrata."

Jeb nodded, unable to put his emotions into words. From the moment he'd seen Sarah again entering the Lapps' barn for church, his lungs hadn't enough air, as though he were breathing through a straw, his chest filled with feathers and his eyes with stars. He'd smiled at Sarah, and she'd smiled back, her round cheeks a lovely shade of pink as she looked him over. Though, of course, Jeb knew pride to be a sin, he'd never been prouder of how his work these past two years had filled out his frame. No more was he the thin, bony scarecrow of his childhood and early teens.

Like Sarah, he had apprenticed away from home. He'd thought he might put down roots in New York State, work with his uncle until he'd sold enough furniture to buy his own farm, but while he'd liked the people there, and some of the girls had certainly caught his attention, none in the past year and a half had matched Sarah. He remembered her as a girl, tiny and tough, her speed and keen eye had made her devastating at recess softball games. Now that tiny, quick-witted girl had become a truly compelling woman. In her time away, she'd acquired a confidence and comfort in her skin that Jeb couldn't turn away from. He wanted to get to know her better, to learn who she was now and how they might fit together, both as adults.

"You're going to have to let Waneta down easy though," Zach continued. "You're not courting with her, are you?"

"Waneta?" Hadn't she been on his team last Saturday for volleyball? They'd barely spoken. "No."

"My sister said that Fannie thought that you were courting with Waneta."

"We're not," Jeb said. "You should tell your sister that gossiping is a sin."

Zach snorted. "That's between Mary and God. Besides, Mary's got a temper, and she punches like the back leg of a mule. I'm not giving her an excuse to use her right hook on me."

"Well, tell your sister to tell all of her friends that I said we weren't courting," Jeb said. "Because we're not. I want to court with Sarah."

They walked around the back of the barn, and one of the other boys waved him over. Jeb spent the next hour or so roughhousing with his friends. It was fun to be home again, and while the marvels of the Englischer world had certainly captured Jeb's imagination for the summer that he had used the money he'd saved from his job to travel all of the way to California, his home was here.

That thought stayed in his heart as he and the other young men fell into an impromptu game of tag. They fooled around until the families that were not staying for the Sing needed help getting their horses from the pasture.

CHAPTER 6

As Fannie followed Waneta from the group of girls, the fragile happiness she'd held in her heart vanished in the clear evidence of Jebediah's disregard for her older sister. Instead of going to the kitchen to help Mrs. Lapp with the cleanup, Waneta led Fannie around the back side of the house and far into the cornfield. Only when the sounds of the other parishioners had faded did Waneta squat down so that she was partially obscured by the thigh-high stalks of green corn.

"Sit," Waneta ordered Fannie.

Fannie obeyed, the seat of her dress dampened by the wet earth. "I'm sorry," Fannie said, reaching for her sister's hand.

"Sorry for what?" Waneta asked. Her brows furrowed together in genuine confusion.

Had Waneta not seen? Fannie wasn't sure if she was grateful or terrified. Certainly Waneta's happiness was important, but not if it was a false happiness. The heartbreak would only be worse if she continued to wait for a courtship that would never happen and then found out the object of her affections loved another at the announcement of the autumn weddings.

Fannie said, "Jeb seems like he's interested in Sarah."

"Sarah, yes," Waneta said. "She is a distraction."

The diffuse fear that had settled beneath Sarah's skin when her sister had first mentioned the courtship sharpened. Waneta could be stubborn, and in her grief at their mamm's illness, it made sense that she would cling to the things she saw as good in her life. "Are you sure…I mean, if Jeb likes Sarah, it's not good to try and push yourself into the middle of that."

"I just need to remind him," Waneta said. "Of his feelings for me, that's what mamm said. You'll help me, won't you?"

"Mamm?" Fannie said. "Daed let you visit her at the hospital?"

"I am an adult, and she's my mamm," Waneta said. "I can visit whenever I like."

A sharp stab of jealousy stole Fannie's breath for a moment. "How…" she managed. "How is she?"

"Good," Waneta said.

"Has she asked after me? Us? The rest of us?"

"She says she loves us all," Waneta said. "And she wants you to help me."

"Of course, I'll help you," Fannie said.

Waneta's face blossomed into a smile. "You're the best sister!" she said, her eyes filled with the same light they'd held in the kitchen just a week ago, when they'd had their soap fight in the kitchen.

Dear God, this must be right, to bring such happiness to my sister.

"Now," Waneta leaned towards the younger girl, a conspiring smile on her face. "Here's what we're going to do."

Fannie let her sister's words wash over her, ignoring the worries that whirled through her mind. When had her sister visited their mamm, considering she spent every day on the farm managing the household tasks? How would the older girl have gotten to the hospital? And how could their mamm support this plan, one spun in deceit that put Waneta's life in danger.

Fannie ignored these questions, only reserving one, the most important one, for when Waneta finished her explanation. "Will you take me with you next time?" Fannie asked. "When you visit mamm?"

Waneta nodded. "Of course."

It was worth it then. Worth any pain to see their mamm whole again.

CHAPTER 7

Eighteen young men and women stayed for the Sing. Mrs. Lapp's living room was too small for such a large group, so they set up battery powered lights at all corners of the barn. In the right corner of the barn, four church benches were set up in a rough square. The gentle lowing of the four cows, black and white Holsteins, resting in their pens after spending the day at pasture, gave the barn had a warm and homey feel.

Mr. Troyer and his wife stood together next to a table laden with plates of leftovers from the Fellowship. Mrs. Troyer waved Sarah over when she entered the barn. Mrs. Troyer was in her mid-twenties and visibly pregnant, her hair the light brown of young wheat. Annie had given Sarah the whole story earlier that afternoon. Mrs. Troyer had taken her baptismal vows without having a successful courtship during her rumspringa and thus hadn't found love until her mid-twenties when Mr. Troyer, a widow from an Amish community in New York State, had come south to Lancaster to escape the memories of the loss of his wife. The pair had hit it off almost immediately, and while they'd skirted tradition a bit in their courtship—seeing each other in secret as adults—the community had looked the other way and had been joyous when the couple announced their marriage last fall.

"Miss Lambright," Mrs. Troyer said, taking the plate of Friendship Bread that Sarah had been carrying. "I hear you and your daed spoke with the Bishop about having you starting to teach in the next term."

"Ja," Sarah said. A tendril of nervousness settled in her gut. Mrs. Beiler had sent a letter on her behalf, but Sarah should have spoken with Mrs. Troyer before the Bishop. "I'm sorry, I should have—"

"It's fine," Mrs. Troyer gave a tight smile that didn't reach her eyes. "I received Mrs. Beiler's letter. She spoke highly of you. I know this isn't a good time to talk, but I'd be happy to speak with you sometime this week. The district elders make the final decision for who teaches, but--"

"I'd love to!" Sarah said. "I want to know all I can about the scholars. I wasn't sure if it was proper to speak with you without speaking with the elders first, but you've been working with the scholars for the past four years, and you really know them. Their hopes, dreams and interests—"

"Ja, ja!" Mrs. Troyer's smile widened into a genuine grin. "I can see you've got the teaching bug, and there aren't any other candidates at this time, and certainly none with your qualifications.

By God's will, I can only see this working out for all of us. I was honestly a bit concerned we wouldn't be able to find someone for the position."

"It would be my honor," Sarah said. "And if I had any chance before the end of the year, I'd love to come to the school and see how you do things, to help ease the transition."

"Wunderbar!" Mrs. Troyer said. "There's simply so much you can learn from a teacher's notes, no matter how detailed I would make them."

"Absolutely," Sarah said.

Sarah was floating on a cloud of happiness as she rejoined her friends for the Sing.

"That looks like it went well," Annie said when Sarah had seated herself on the bench.

"I think so," Sarah said, modestly. "Where's Ruth?"

Annie leaned in and whispered in Sarah's ear, "She said she was getting something from the kitchen, but I'm sure she's conspiring with Mark behind the barn. Those two are as thick as thieves. I'm looking towards an announcement in the fall."

Sarah was a bit surprised that Ruth would be so blatant in her questioning. Of course, she'd always been a straightforward sort. Sarah had wondered if Ruth would find someone who admired her direct nature, and if she and Mark had fallen in love…

Sarah smiled, truly content. "What about you?" she asked Annie. "Is there anyone in your life?"

Before Annie could answer, the barn door opened, and a group of young men came in. Sarah spotted Jeb, as always in stride with Zach.

The young men were coming into the room in groups of two and three. She caught sight of Zach at the food table trying to snag a Friendship muffin from the plate of Church Fellowship leftovers.

"Not now, Zach!" Mrs. Troyer said, slapping his hand away. "Didn't you eat two full plates at lunch?"

"I'm a growing boy," Zach said, unrepentant.

"Only in your belly, if you don't watch yourself," Mrs. Troyer said with a laugh.

Jeb and Zach sat down on the bench perpendicular to the one where Sarah, Annie and Ruth were already sitting.

Zach, unsurprisingly, started the conversation, "So how was life in Ephrata, Sarah?"

Sarah smiled, less at the question and more at the expression of rapt attention on Jeb's face. "Gutt," she said. "I loved working with the scholars." Feeling especially bold, she added, "I might have stayed if I'd found someone, but…"

Zach glanced over to his friend, "So you aren't courting with anyone yet?"

Annie laughed, "She's hardly had time!"

"Nee," Sarah said.

"Well, I'm sure someone will present himself," Zach said as the barn door opened again, letting in a rush of cool spring air and three more young women, Rachel, Katie and Waneta.

The three young women walked in together, Katie and Rachel close together, their arms almost touching as they laughed. Though Waneta smiled with the other two girls, she looked very much an outsider. Maybe it was because Waneta was older, almost twenty, while the other two girls had been a year behind Sarah and were now eighteen. Sarah wondered if Waneta had any close friends among the other, unmarried girls. She'd never seemed close to the women her own age, and most had announced their marriages in the fall, Sarah assumed, either that or they had left, perhaps never to return. Sarah felt for Waneta, who had not only lost her mamm, but also been left behind by the girls her own age, as well.

Waneta separated from the other two girls as she approached the benches. "Annie! Ruth!" She waved cheerfully. Glancing at her friend, Annie's had managed a smile, but her lips were tight and the return wave she gave far more reserved than usual. "Waneta," she said. "I thought you were going back home this afternoon with your family."

"Nee," Waneta said. "Mr. Troyer offered me and my sister a ride back with them."

"Your sister?" Sarah was surprised. At fifteen, Fannie was not yet old enough to begin her Rumspringa and thus too young to join the other unbaptized youths for the Sing.

"Daed and the boys can get themselves to bed, and Fannie's volunteered to stay behind and help Mrs. Lapp with her kinner. It works out well. Fannie's wanted to get out of the house, and she loves kinner."

Sarah nodded. It made sense, but there was a tightness in Waneta's shoulders that made Sarah think the other girl might be nervous, though Sarah couldn't imagine why. There was plenty of room on the other side of the bench, but Waneta squeezed herself in between Sarah and the boys. "How was Ephrata?" she asked Sarah.

"We were just talking about that," Ruth said. "Sarah's really found her calling to teach."

"Teach?" Waneta raised her eyebrows. "I heard you were doing an apprenticeship, but not that you'd taken to it so well. You don't want to get married?"

"Of course she wants to get married!" Annie cut in. "You can be a teacher and married. Look at Mrs. Troyer."

"Well..." Waneta gave a slow nod. "Of course you *can*...but it is more difficult once you have kinner of your own I think. It's a good thing if you have a calling. God gives us each gifts and commandments. It's up to us to listen and follow." There was a light to Waneta's eyes...something like victory. "I think it's really incredible that you feel so strongly about teaching our youth."

Sarah stamped down a spike of violent anger at the other girl's words. Waneta wasn't wrong, not exactly. It was difficult to maintain a schoolhouse and a family. Even Mrs. Troyer was abandoning the first in favor of the unborn child she carried. At least for a time.

If Sarah and Jeb married, would Sarah also have to abandon her dream? Would Jeb even want to court with a woman whose heart was pulled in two directions?

At that moment, Mrs. Troyer tapped her spoon against the side of her glass and said in a clear voice, "Let's begin the Sing."

Though their voices were light with hope and fellowship, the song was not enough to lift Sarah's heart. She couldn't even meet Jebediah's gaze. Instead, she looked up at dark corner of the barn ceiling, praying in unformed thoughts for some scrap of guidance until the music ended.

CHAPTER 8

Jebediah was grateful he'd have almost forty minutes with Sarah in the buggy on the way to their homes because he hadn't had a moment to speak with Sarah since the very beginning of the Sing. It was as though Waneta had an endless fascination with Ephrata, the minutiae of teaching, and any other topic of conversation that she might be able to rope Sarah into having. Jeb had nothing to be angry about. Waneta's behavior had been entirely proper, and some of her stories had even wrung a laugh from Jeb and other nearby youths.

At the same time, the situation was more than a little frustrating. Had Zach not mentioned the rumor of Jeb and Waneta courting earlier, Jeb would have been inclined to assume the entire situation was merely a case of poor timing and over enthusiasm on Waneta's part. Now, Zach's questioning had made Jeb suspicious, but Waneta didn't seem to be harboring a hidden crush. In fact, today she'd hardly spoken with Jebediah.

After they had finished consolidating the leftovers onto two plates and stacking the rest of the used dishware to return to the Lapps', Waneta finally left to get her sister. A greater blessing,

Sarah's friends followed Waneta into the house, giving Jeb a precious moment alone with Sarah on the porch.

"Sarah—" Jeb started at the same time Sarah said, "Jebediah—"

Both youths burst out laughing, and suddenly it was comfortable between them. "You first, please," Sarah said.

"I know this is rather abrupt," Jeb said, his words tumbling into each other in his nervousness. "But I'd like very much a chance to get to know you better—to court—if you feel—"

"Ja," Sarah said, her gaze soft.

Jebediah was caught with a strong urge to take Sarah into his arms, but he couldn't on the Lapps' porch on a Church Sunday.

Instead, he extended his hand. Sarah took it, and for a brief moment, their hands clasped.

The screen door opened, and Waneta poked her head out. "Sarah, where are you?"

Jeb quickly dropped Sarah's hand, his cheeks hot as he stepped away from Sarah.

"Oh, there you are," Waneta said. "Mrs. Lapp is very tired, so it'd be best to get those plates in as soon as possible. Sarah, you'll stay and help us get the dishes washed, right? I don't want to leave them for poor Mrs. Lapp in the morning. She's practically falling down on her feet."

"Of course, of course," Sarah said and followed Waneta into the house. Jebediah followed. When he'd dropped his pile of plates off in the kitchen, Waneta again took charge, asking, "Jeb, shouldn't you see to getting your buggy ready for the road?"

"Ja," Jeb said. It was foolish to want to stay in the kitchen with the other women. Foolish and improper. Still, he couldn't help feeling like he'd been banished, and that, somehow, he'd lost ground in a battle he hadn't known he was fighting.

CHAPTER 9

Though Fannie usually enjoyed playing with kinner, Waneta's plan had Fannie too nauseated to have fun. Wouldn't spooking the horse put her sister, or some other innocent, in harm's way? By the time the kinner were put to bed, Fannie's head was pounding, and the back of her tongue tasted like acid.

"Are you okay, Fannie," Mrs. Lapp asked as they walked back to the kitchen to finish up with the dishes. "You look ill."

"I'm fine," Fannie said. "I must have eaten too much." The lie felt like sawdust in her mouth.

Dear God, forgive me, she prayed. Lying was a sin. Allowing her sister to put herself in harm's way, wasn't that also a sin? Was it selfish to want to see her mamm again?

For all have sinned, and come short of the glory of God...

They worked in silence in the kitchen for a while, Fannie elbows deep in sudsy water, before she finally had the courage to speak.

"How do you know if you're being selfish?" Fannie asked.

"Selfish?" Mrs. Lapp stacked a serving plate into the strainer. "Is that what's been bothering you? How do you think you're being selfish?"

As much as Fannie wanted to share her secret, share how difficult it had been for all of them since her mamm had been taken away to the hospital, she couldn't betray her sister's trust. "It's nothing," Fannie said.

"I see."

They worked in silence again, until the last of the afternoon dishes was washed and dried. Fannie opened the drain and let the now grey water swirl downwards. She'd refill it again for after the Sing, when the rest of the plates were returned.

"Danki, Fannie," Mrs. Lapp said. "Do you mind if I sit?"

"Of course," Fannie said. She felt bad to have had Mrs. Lapp standing for so long. "You don't have to do anything else. I can handle the rest."

Mrs. Lapp walked to the kitchen table and pulled out one of the wooden chairs. It had a lovely cushion on the seat, sewn from what looked like remnants of quilting fabric.

"About your question," Mrs. Lapp said, leaning back on the seat and closing her eyes. "I've never been good at knowing what's truly selfish or selfless. As human beings, I think we're more selfish than not. The question isn't are we truly selfless, but if our actions are making the world better for others or are we only serving our own interests? But that can be difficult to see. Even the cleanest water will run grey if muddied enough. That's why we pray, to drain that darkness from us so that we can be filled anew."

Fannie nodded. Dear God, she whispered in her mind. Please show me the best way to help my family be happy again.

It was a true prayer, and an honest one. Though Fannie received no answers, she felt herself more at peace than she had the entire day.

The front door opened, and the sound of laughing voices sounded from down the hall.

Zach and another boy, one of the apprentices whose name Fannie didn't remember, handed Fannie a stack of plates. Fannie took it. Two more boys came in with plates stacked high with leftovers. Fannie pointed to the roll of tinfoil on the kitchen counter. "And then put those in the refrigerator." The older girls then took the responsibility for organizing things from Fannie, a relief and at the same time a burden when Waneta finally came inside. She chatted with the boys a little, waving them off, and then glancing inside the dish strainer beside the sink, picked up one of the tomato knives.

"Come on," Waneta said, waving Fannie towards the living

room. Fannie went first, and had seated herself uncomfortably on the sofa when Waneta joined her.

"When I give the signal," Waneta whispered. "You shout out something to distract everyone. I'm going to use this pin." She fingered along the back of her bonnet and pulled out a wickedly sharp needle. It was long and thick, the sort used for sewing heavy canvas.

"Are you sure this is safe?" Fannie asked.

"It's fine," Waneta said. "Now you stay with the Troyers until it's time to go."

Fannie did as she was told, the nausea she'd been fighting earlier rising back in her throat again. She wanted to vomit. She wanted to run away into the field before anything bad happened. She wanted to cry. This past year, she'd grown so tall so quickly that she felt like a tiny child in an awkward, adult frame. She hated it. For a brief, agonizing moment, she hated her sister for making her do these things, but she couldn't hate Waneta. For all of their childhood, Waneta had been the strong one. She'd held the family together when their mamm had been sent away the first time, when Waneta was eleven and Fannie only eight. Now Waneta was showing that strength again to risk her life for the person she loved. The man who had promised to court with her.

If that's what had truly happened, a hateful, doubting voice whispered in Fannie's mind.

Too soon the dishes were finished, the leftovers put away, and the youths dispersing to their buggies. Fannie followed Waneta, the cheerful farewells sounding like dirges in Fannie's ears.

The moon was almost full, bathing the driveway and fields in a milky light. Maybe Waneta had changed her mind, Fannie thought with increasing hope as they approached their own buggy.

Mrs. Troyer leaned on her husband's arm as she walked. "I think I may not be able to do that again, at least not so late," the pregnant woman said.

"Sarah's waving for us!" Waneta suddenly exclaimed. "Come on, Fannie."

"Do you think she wants me?" Mrs. Troyer asked. "I didn't see anything."

"We'd best go," Mr. Troyer said.

Fannie's stomach sank. Whatever Waneta planned with the horse, it wasn't a good idea to have a pregnant woman nearby. "I think she just wants Waneta," Fannie said. "You should go and sit down in the buggy."

"Nonsense, Fannie. I'm pregnant, not dying," Mrs. Troyer said with a laugh. "Besides, it's my job to chaperone you young people."

Waneta strode off ahead of them. "Sarah!" she shouted.

Sarah looked back at them. "Ja?"

Jeb, who had been standing behind Sarah, looked over at them too, a brief expression of annoyance washing over his features. Dear heavens, Fannie realized, Waneta didn't have a chance.

"Didn't you wave us over?" Waneta asked.

"Nee."

"She didn't," Jeb said.

"I'm sorry," Waneta said, continuing towards them.

"We should go," Fannie said, waving her sister back. "We're very sorry."

"It's nothing, Fannie," Sarah said, nodding to Fannie. While Fannie and Jeb were of equal height, Sarah had to look up to meet Fannie's gaze. "Mr. and Mrs. Troyer," Sarah continued, nodding to the teacher and her husband.

"So you didn't wave us over?" Mrs. Troyer asked.

"I'm sorry," Sarah said. "I don't know what—"

Waneta, forgotten, stood at the rump of the horse. She'd removed the pin from her bonnet. It shone dangerously in the moonlight. She raised her eyebrows, giving Fannie a pointed look.

Terror closed Fannie's throat. In normal circumstances, she hated putting herself in the center of attention, and now, Waneta's plan seemed even more foolish than it had this afternoon when she'd explained it. Someone could get hurt, or worse.

"Now," Waneta mouthed.

Catching sight of Fannie's expression, Sarah asked, "Fannie, are you okay?"

Fannie burst into tears.

At that moment, the horse reared, teeth bared and ears flat against his head as he started to run, dragging the buggy behind him. Jeb and Mr. Troyer started after it. Inside the buggy, Deacon Yoder grabbed at the reins, trying to slow the horse.

Waneta screamed and grabbed at Jeb's sleeve as he passed. "Help me!" She held her left hand up. Dark lines of blood ran from a deep gash in her palm.

It was exactly as Fannie had feared, and now Waneta was hurt and crying. "Please," Waneta said, her gaze locking with Jeb's.

Runaway horse forgotten, Jeb tapped helplessly at his trousers before taking off his jacket and holding out the sleeve. "Use this."

Waneta took the jacket with an almost reverent expression and wrapped it around her hand. "Danki," she said, looking into his eyes. Before Jeb could respond, she closed the short distance between them and leaned against him, resting her head against his chest as though suddenly exhausted.

Fannie dropped to her knees, wiping tears and snot from her face with her sleeve. She wanted, more than anything, to run to her sister's side, but she couldn't move.

"Are you okay, child?" Mrs. Troyer rested her palm on Fannie's shoulder. "It'll be okay, Fannie. They're getting the old girl calmed down right now, and your sister will be fine, you'll see. Hands bleed a lot, but it looks like a shallow cut. It was just an accident. God will see it right."

Fannie wished she had the strength of the older woman's convictions, but the horse had been spooked by design, not accident. It was only God's will that the buggy had been facing down the driveway, or else the horse in her fear and pain might have run into a field or thrown himself into the farmhouse itself.

"Danki," Waneta murmured again and again against Jeb's chest. "You saved me."

It was all wrong.

Dear God, help me. Fannie prayed. *Help us.*

CHAPTER 10

Once the horse was calmed, arrangements were made to get Waneta to the hospital. Though Sarah would have preferred to ride with Jeb, she agreed to ride home with the Troyers.

Before leaving, Mrs. Troyer, who had taken a first-aid and CPR class before she'd begun teaching, took a look at Waneta's cut and said that it looked too deep simply to bandage. "You'll need to get her to the hospital for stitches before the tissue along the edges begins to die. Otherwise, it'll have a nasty scar, and she won't be able to use that hand so well."

"I thought you said it was shallow," Fannie exclaimed. The poor girl had taken Waneta's injury far more to heart than Waneta herself, her lower lip quivering as she spoke, shoulders hunched and hands grasped tightly together in her lap. "Isn't it just that hands bleed a lot?"

"In most cases," Mrs. Troyer said. "To be honest, I'm shocked the cut went so deep. Did you cut it on the buggy?"

Waneta nodded.

"Well, it's out of our hands. You'll have to be more careful of the back side of horses," Mrs. Troyer added, patting Waneta gently on the knee. "You should at least wash the wound now, as much as it will hurt. You don't want an infection. And make sure they update your tetanus."

"I will," Waneta said.

Zach and Jeb took the buggy together to the nearest emergency payphone, which had been set up for the Amish ten years back near a local pharmacy. When Waneta was led back to the house, she looked briefly disappointed to be separated from Jebediah.

Jealousy is an ugly trait, Sarah reminded herself.

The ride back was quiet, punctuated by the buggy's rattling, the gentle clip-clop of the horse's hooves and eventually Mrs. Troyer's quiet snores.

Sarah didn't get home until after midnight. She did her best to open the door quietly so as not to wake the rest of the family, but their dog Bandit must have recognized the sound of her footsteps because he started barking as soon as she stepped in.

"Sarah, is that you?" Her daed's voice sounded from up the stairs.

"Ja! There was an accident at the Sing and Waneta cut herself," Sarah explained quickly. It was too dark in the house to see beyond her nose. Sarah felt along the wall for the battery powered lantern. In her childhood, they'd used only gas lanterns, but after a family in a neighboring district had burned down their barn when one had accidentally been left, still lit, next to an open bale of hay, Sarah's daed had switched to battery powered lights for anything portable.

Sarah was grateful for the convenience as she turned it on. The battery would soon need to be changed, she noted as dull orange light shone dimly from the bulb.

"Well, get yourself to bed," her daed shouted. "Rooster'll start screaming before dawn."

Sarah nodded, knowing that he couldn't hear the gesture Bandit met her at the top of the stairs. Within fifteen minutes, she had changed, brushed her teeth and fallen asleep.

Dawn came far too soon. Sarah's eyes were heavy, and her eyelids gummed with sleep when the rooster started his pre-dawn screeching. She hadn't missed that rooster. Yawning, she sat up. Her brothers were already moving around in the next door rooms.

While Sarah had always wanted a sister, she as grateful to have her own room, unlike her brothers who had to share. She stood up, stretched, and began to root around the dresser for clothes.

A gentle knock sounded at her door.

"I'm dressed," Sarah called out.

The door opened, and her mamm strode in. "Gutt," she said with a smile. "The school board agreed to meet with you this afternoon. There's also a young man, Jebediah, who seems to be quite friendly. You went to school with him I remember. He's a solid lad, and one with a good work ethic, or at least that's what the man apprenticed with said in his letters. Apparently he is going to call on your daed tomorrow morning. The young man seems keen to try his hand at mending the chair leg in the living room." Sarah's district held more firmly than others to the idea that courtships should not be mentioned directly to the parents before a firm wedding announcement, but a polite man did try to ask some form of permission, as it seemed Jeb was doing.

Sarah's face broke into a wide grin. "Wunderbar!"

Sarah's mamm laughed. "I assured him we had no problem with him calling on our home, provided it wasn't a bother to the family." Her eyes narrowed with mirth. "You're certain this Jebediah's calling here won't trouble you?"

"Not at all."

"Well then, Atlee is rifling around the chicken coop this morning for eggs, and Willis has been sent for milk from the Umbles, so why don't you join me in the kitchen. When you're ready."

"Ja," Sarah said. As her mamm turned to go, Sarah walked to

her. "Mamm?"

"Ja?"

Sarah wrapped her arms around her mamm, pulling her into a tight hug. "I love you."

"Are you okay?" Her mamm returned the hug, rubbing a slow circle between her daughter's shoulder blades.

"I was just thinking of Waneta's family...and..."

"I understand." Sarah's mamm held her daughter tighter. "I'm not one to spread nasty gossip and I'm sure you've heard all manner of tales already. Those kinner are having a difficult time, and I don't believe their daed is one for talking to them about difficult things. Or having them along when he visits his wife. It can't be good for them, but I've no place to judge. Be kind is all I'm saying. What you see of any person is just the surface. Only God knows the pain we carry inside."

Sarah nodded, her cheek rubbing against the soft fabric of her mamm's dress. "I had no plans of spreading rumors," she said.

"I know you wouldn't. You're a good child. That said, be careful of the oldest girl. I think Waneta carries more of her mamm's ways than the others. It's a burden she's had to bear because she's the oldest, but some loads are enough to break the strongest back. Let alone being carried on the back of a child."

"I understand."

"Gutt. I'll see you downstairs for dawn prayers."

And with that, Sarah was left to choose her dress for the day. All thoughts of Waneta's troubles were lost in the anticipation of her afternoon meeting with the district school board. No matter how good her references, if she didn't impress these men, she'd have no chance at getting the position. Today was laundry day, which meant she only had one good dress left clean. She took it from the closet where she'd hung it just days ago and laid it on the bed. Though she'd taken a full bath for church yesterday, it would be best to do so again. Sarah wanted to make the best impression.

And then tomorrow, Jeb would call. She had her parents' approval for the courtship, and while she hardly knew him, she had been impressed with the calm way he'd handled both the spooked horse and Waneta. God must have brought Sarah and Jebediah home at the same time for a reason. She prayed it was because they had been meant to find each other.

CHAPTER 11

The situation, while serious, was hardly life threatening, and an ambulance would be an unnecessary expense for the community who pooled their resources to pay for their parishioners' medical care, so a taxi was called to take Waneta to the hospital. Jeb and Zach decided to spend the night in the Lapp's spare room and return the church buggy after Zach drove Jeb home in the morning.

Zach drove the buggy, and Jeb sat beside him, enjoying the crisp bite of early spring. Dew glistened on the green corn and browning stalks of wheat that lined the road. The Lapps had foisted, with little protest, a hearty breakfast on the two young men, and bellies full, they rattled pleasantly down the road, the peace of the morning broken only by the occasional Englischer car zipping past.

"Star's as placid a mare as I've ever seen," Zach said, after a bit. "What do you think spooked her so badly?"

"I don't know," Jeb said. He'd been wondering through the night. In his dreams even, he watched Star rear upwards, the flaring of her nostrils seeming large and horrifying in the throes of his slumber. "It was something behind her, for sure," he mused.

"Her ears were going straight back and she ran straight away. Waneta was lucky the buggy didn't run her over."

"Maybe something bit her? Star I mean, not Waneta. "

"Ja," Jeb agreed. "Though it's early for mosquitoes and too late for flies. Besides, horses are used to flies. Could have been a hornet, I guess."

"Maybe." Zach didn't look convinced. "I'm more surprised Waneta was cut like that."

"What do you mean?"

"I mean, if she was trying to get away, wouldn't she have jumped away from the buggy? And if so, how could she have cut herself like that? Unless it was deliberate."

Jeb shrugged. "I can't imagine why she'd cut herself on purpose."

"Well, she sure seemed happy enough in your arms."

Jeb laughed. "My arms are nice, I guess, but not worth going to the hospital for. Besides, you saw how upset Waneta was."

"I saw how upset Fannie was. You'd have thought she'd been the one who cut herself!"

"It was just an accident," Jeb said. "I'm not reading anymore into it than that. Besides, Waneta and her sister have it hard enough with their mamm, and now this. I should call on Waneta, just to see how she's doing."

"If you don't, I'm sure she'll find a way to call on you."

Jebediah didn't like this suspicious side to his best friend. "Just leave it alone," he said.

Zach shook his head, but let the subject drop. "So, I heard you're going to call on Sarah's daed today…"

"I've asked Sarah to court with me," Jeb said, his cheeks warming a bit.

"Really!" Zach shifted both reins into his right hand before using his left to give Jeb a firm punch in the shoulder. "Good for you! When did you get a chance? It didn't look like Waneta was going to leave either of you alone long enough to get a word together."

"I said let it go," Jeb said, anger hardening his tone. "And you should keep both hands firm on those reins. We have no idea what set Star off in the first place."

"Whatever it was, I doubt it's going to bother any of us today." That was the last Zach said on the subject.

It was well after ten by the time Jebediah made it back to his parents' farm. His daed had already left to work at the factory, leaving the rest of the family to tend their small wheat field. Jeb's family farm was smaller than most in the district, with no room for cows. They had a tiny pasture for the two horses, and a barn for them to retreat to in cold weather. Half of the barn doubled as storage, one small corner reserved for their daed's whittling, which was his true passion. Jeb wished he'd inherited some of his daed's talent. In less than half an hour with his tools, Jeb's daed could turn a simple, discarded chunk of wood into a fat raccoon, or a cow, or a smiling pig. Jeb had spent much of his childhood with his sisters and brothers making up increasingly fantastical stories with the animals their daed had carved. Only two of his sisters had inherited their daed's talent, his oldest, married and living in a neighboring district, and the second youngest, Ruthie, age nine, whom everyone called Summer for her bright blond hair and even brighter smile.

To Jeb's surprise, Summer ran from the garden to greet him, her prayer kapp tied tightly to her head by her their mamm who knew her daughter's penchant for losing anything not directly attached to her.

"Jeb!" Summer shouted, rocking forward on her toes and waving both arms over her head as though trying to bring in a wayward ship.

"Shouldn't you be in school?" Jeb asked.

"Mrs. Troyer was feeling ill, and they couldn't get a substitute for more than half of the day, so they sent us home after lunch. I was hoping that we'd get to meet the new teacher. She's just returned from Ephrata, isn't she?"

"Sarah," Jeb said. "You'll like her."

Sarah shrugged.

Jeb slowed the buggy and parked it on the edge of the driveway next to the house. Climbing down, he first saw to Star, getting her out of the harness.

Summer ran to Jeb's side. "I'm glad you're back, but you missed breakfast!"

Summer's nose had a bump at the base from accident last year where she'd somehow climbed up onto the roof of the barn, "To get a better angle on the horses," she'd explained later when she's slipped while climbing down and landed directly on her face. They'd done their best to set the nose before rushing her by buggy to the neighbors' with a phone, but the bone had never quite healed right. It hadn't kept Summer from doing foolish and daring things, however, and while Jeb, like the rest of his family, scolded her for her rashness, in his heart she was his favorite.

"I ate at the Lapps'," Jeb said, freeing Star from the buggy. The horse was as placid as always, plodding behind him with the slightest tug of the reins towards the barn. When he got to the barn, he filled the trough with water and hay, still chatting with his sister.

"I'm glad you ate already," Summer said with a solemn nod. "Because I had your pork fritters."

"Pork fritters?"

"The Zooks slaughtered one of their pigs last week, don't you remember?" Summer kicked at a rock on the ground, her face screwed up in exasperation. "They gave us a cut of it yesterday at Church to thank daed for the carving he did for their son Peter."

"Peter...right..." "Can you fill Star's trough with some hay?" Jeb asked.

"Ja," Summer said and ran off ahead. When he'd caught up, a lump of loose hay filled the bottom of the trough. Star pricked her ears and walked towards it.

"Right," Summer said, decisively. "Come talk to mamm. She was worried when you didn't come back last night though she said she isn't going to say anything because it's your Rumspringa, and she doesn't want to see like she's being nosy."

Jeb burst out laughing. Summer couldn't keep a thought to herself, so, of course, his mamm had meant for him to know that she had been worried. "I'll apologize," Jeb said. "Where is she? In the kitchen?"

"Nee, she went to check on the washer in the back room. The extension cord to the generator might have a short in it, she said, because it's been acting fussy the last week. That's what she *said*, but I think she just wanted me out of the house while she stared at the washer." Summer wrinkled her nose. "We're going to be hanging the sheets as soon as they're done."

Summer followed Jeb into the house, a cotton sack of string beans clutched in her right hand. She slipped her left into her older brother's, and together they climbed the steps of the porch and walked into the house.

"Mamm!" Summer shouted as soon as Jeb had opened the door.

A muffled voice sounded from the back of the house. "Jeb! Are you back?"

"Ja," Jeb made a quick pace down the hall to the back room where his mamm squatted next to the washing machine. Wisps of steel-grey hair clung to her neck. The machine was off, and his mamm looked up from it with an expression of profound frustration on her plump, round face. "Heavens, I don't want to be hand scrubbing these clothes all day," she said. "Where were you? You and Zachariah didn't get into any trouble, did you?"

Though Zach and Jeb's families had been neighbors for longer than Jeb had been alive, since the boys had become teenagers and Zach had convinced Jeb to travel across country in an RV with him and some Englischer friends, Jeb's mamm had been convinced that Zach had a nose for trouble. In truth, Zach had gotten Jeb out of more trouble than the opposite.

"Nee, mamm," Jeb said and explained the night's events.

His mamm stood, the furrow between her brows deepening as he spoke. "Something spooked Star?"

"Ja. We're still not sure as to what, but horses sometimes spook."

"Hmm…"

When Jeb had finished explaining, his mamm folded his arms over her chest and said, "We can't leave that family in that state!"

Shocked at the fervor of his mamm's words, Jeb asked, "Why? I mean, I know her mamm—"

"It's not just her mamm. There are too many secrets in that family, and Waneta's had to carry the bulk of them. I've asked the Bishop to speak with their daed, but he doesn't see any need to meddle, unasked, into another family's affairs." Jeb's mamm clapped her hands together and shook her head, nose wrinkling with exactly the same expression of distaste that Summer gave lima beans. "It's exactly his place to meddle in other people's affairs, when meddling needs to be done. That's a family crying for help. Englischers may live their lives in separate bubbles, not giving a care for their neighbors, but that's not the lives God ordained for us Amish." She shook her head again. "And while it's not my place to dictate the Bishop's responsibilities that doesn't mean we can't help. I'll speak with Rebecca at Wednesday's quilting group. We'll make sure that family has proper support. Now, can you go into your daed's part of the barn and look for the spare cord? You've always had more patience for his system of 'organizing' things than I have. If this doesn't work, we're going to have to use the washboards instead."

"Ja, mamm," Jeb said and hurried towards the barn.

"Can I start with the washboard now," Summer asked cheerfully.

"If you like," their mamm said with a sigh.

The rest of the day kept him too busy to think about either Waneta or Sarah. It was only at dinner that he realized that he hadn't mentioned either Sarah or his plans for the morrow to either his mamm or daed.

"May I use the buggy tomorrow," Jeb asked as they were finishing dessert.

"If you want," his daed said. "Where are you going?"

"Mr. Lambright has a chair that needs mending."

"And a pretty daughter you might be courting," Jeb's daed took a second cinnamon bun and pulled a gooey hunk off to pop in his mouth. "It's not my place to know, but Sarah's a dependable girl with a good heart. Word is out that she's going to be replacing Mrs. Troyer in the Fall at the school."

Was she? Jeb realized how little he knew about Sarah. He definitely liked her, but if they had any chance of a future together, he would need to learn more of her dreams and interests; otherwise he might as well court with Waneta, or any other girl. "That's good," Jeb said. "I know she apprenticed in Ephrata with another teacher."

"Yes, in the proper way," his daed said, eating another piece of the pastry. "Some of the younger set in other districts are learning in Englischer colleges instead of doing an apprenticeship, and while there's no shame in that, you can't harvest a proper Amish education from an Englischer root, any more than an apple tree will give you peaches in the spring."

"Ja, ja," his mamm agreed. "I know Mrs. Troyer will be happy to leave the school in good hands. She was worried they might have to find someone from outside of the district. None of the young girls around here have any interest in teaching."

"Sarah does," Jeb said with conviction, though born of where he wasn't sure. "She's very kind and diligent woman."

"Just what one looks for in a teacher," his daed said, and then in a softer voice, muffled in part by his chewing, he whispered, "And a wife."

CHAPTER 12

Over the protests of the other adults, Fannie went with Waneta to the hospital. She couldn't stand to leave her sister alone, some part of her fearing that if Waneta went alone to the hospital, Fannie might never see her older sister again. Mr. Lapp had offered, rather strenuously, to join them, but Waneta insisted that she would be fine. Fannie stayed at her sister's side for the long taxi ride to the hospital Emergency Room.

While Fannie had had all her yearly checkups with the local doctor who served their community--a straight-backed elderly Amish man turned Mennonite, who spoke in soft, friendly Pennsylvania Dutch and reinforced his diagnosis with common adages that reminded Fannie vaguely of her grandmother who had died when Fannie was just four-- she'd never been to a true Englischer hospital before. An ambulance had arrived just as their taxi had dropped them at the main entrance, all flashing red urgency and noise. Passing through an automatic roundabout, similar to the automatic doors of the Target where her mamm sometimes took them to shop for bulk items, Fannie felt like a horse being pushed through a chute. Inside was quieter at least, a sprawling room of shining white, broken only by the sharp angles of the wooden reception desk. The light seemed too sharp and steady to be healthful, the floors shiny white swirled with gray and smelling of antiseptic.

Waneta walked to the reception desk, Fannie a step behind her. The receptionist was a brown-skinned woman with glasses balanced precariously on her wide, flat nose. "Gut-en-owen," she said in poorly accented Pennsylvania Dutch.

Fannie's eyebrows shot up in shock. "You speak our language?" she said in Pennsylvania Dutch.

"Glee," the receptionist said, holding two fingers to indicate a small amount. She switched to English. "One of my neighbors is Amish," she explained. "So I picked up a few words." Her gaze skimmed over the pair of them, resting on Waneta, still holding her hand to her chest where she'd wrapped it in the sleeve of Jeb's coat. "Did you hurt your hand?"

Waneta nodded. Fannie said, "She did, on the buggy.

It's cut and will need stitches, that's what Mrs. Troyer said. And to update her tetanus."

"Your Mrs. Troyer seems like a bright woman. How old are you, Miss?"

"Bechler." Waneta said. "Waneta Bechler."

"That's lovely, Miss. Bechler. Why don't you give me your name and address? No phone I suppose…and someone will call you back to be admitted." The receptionist smiled, her teeth glinting white against the deep purple of her lipstick.

"Danki," Fannie said.

They sat. On the wall in front of them, an Englischer television showing what looked like some kind of complex metal contraption for lifting weights. An overly excited Englischer man who was embarrassingly stripped down to a form fitting pair of black shorts and a t-shirt that hugged his chest and bared shockingly muscular arms, pointed at the machine and while the screen flashed, "Seventeen minutes a day!"

Fannie averted her gaze, covering her mouth with her hand to muffle her laughter.

Eventually, a nurse called Waneta back, and Fannie followed, listening without speaking as Waneta's arm was wrapped in a blood pressure cuff, and the nurse put a plastic clip on the index finger of her uninjured hand. The line on the machine it was connected to jumping as the machine beeped.

"Looks good," the nurse said. "Can you show me your injury?"

"Ja," Waneta gently unwound the jacket sleeve from her palm and held it out. The area around the wound was puffy and red. "We cleaned it at the house."

"How did this happen? Was it a kitchen knife?"

"Nee!" Fannie cut in before Waneta could speak, surprised that the nurse had guessed so wrong. "It was the buggy."

"Buggy?"

Waneta explained how she had gotten the injury. The nurse looked pursed her lips as Waneta spoke, her gaze flitting between the two girls as Waneta spun her tale.

"Is that how it happened?" the nurse asked Fannie when Waneta had finished.

"I don't know," Fannie said. "I was too far away to see things exactly."

Waneta narrowed her eyes, and for a moment, she looked furious.

"I'm sure that's right," Fannie added quickly.

"I see," the nurse said. She turned to Waneta. "You're lucky that this cut was clean. Usually with an uneven piece of metal, the wound is more jagged and harder to stitch."

"So you can fix it?" Fannie asked.

"Oh yes. Though it's easier to treat things if we know exactly what happened."

"I've told you exactly what happened," Waneta said sharply.

"Well then, we'll admit you and have one of the residents stitch that up. You'll need antibiotics and if there was any rusted metal involved, an update to your tetanus. You wouldn't happen to know when you last had that shot, would you?"

Waneta shook her head.

"That's no problem. Why don't you two sit back down,

and we'll see about getting that fixed up? I'm assuming you'll be billing this. That's what you Amish usually do."

"Ja," Waneta said. "Danki."

"Okay, I'll just need to speak with you for a few more moments on your own, if that's okay?" the nurse looked at Fannie, who bit her lip and locked gazes with Waneta.

"It's fine," Waneta said.

Fannie returned to the waiting room and stared, exhausted, at the flashing television. A kitchen knife? Her memory returned, in spite of her best efforts to ignore it, to the knife she'd seen her sister slip into the pocket of her apron in the Lapps' kitchen before the Sing. Had she cut herself? The thought was horrifying. Her sister had injured herself and then lied about it.

The advertisement blurred in Fannie's vision as she tried to hold back her tears.

Waneta was furious when she returned to the waiting room. "The nerve of that woman," she muttered to herself, her hands in tight fists.

"Are you sure you shouldn't be keeping your hand closed like that?" Fannie asked.

"Next time I say what happened, you just agree with me, do you understand?"

"I can't lie," Fannie said.

"It's not a lie," Waneta said. "You just don't know what you saw." Her tone softened. "Why don't you lean against my shoulder for a bit and try to get some sleep? I know you're tired."

"I'm fine," Fannie said. It was another hour before Waneta was called back to have the wound stitched. They waited, the fingertips of Waneta's uninjured hands rubbing circles and figure eights into the fabric of Jeb's now bloodied jacket, while Fannie drifted in and out of sleep. Though they sat together, the distance between them seemed as far as the sun and the moon, and Fannie cursed herself for her doubts, even as the screams of the horse and visions of her sister's blood chased the younger girl through her dreams.

The next day, Waneta called Fannie to her room. Her hand was wrapped in a thick bandage, and on her night table sat a full bottle of prescription painkillers from the hospital pharmacy. "Do you need me to help you with the bottle?" Fannie asked.

"I'm fine," Waneta said. "The pain isn't that bad, but I'm going to need another favor," she said.

"But—"

Waneta laughed. It sounded false. "It's nothing too difficult, I promise. I just need you to drive the buggy for me tomorrow morning. "We're going to visit Sarah."

"Sarah?" Fannie's stomach churned. "I don't think we should bother her."

"Nonsense. I overheard one of the girls from the Sing, saying that Jebediah would be over Sarah's house this afternoon to do some repair work for her daed. She thought he might be courting with her, but I let her know that wasn't the case."

"But—you don't know," Fannie said.

"Mamm said it doesn't matter."

"Mamm? When did you talk to mamm?"

"It doesn't matter. The point is, all I have to do is get him to notice me again. Sarah wants to be a teacher, not a wife. He'll figure it out soon enough, and when he does, it'll be best if I'm there to comfort him."

Waneta spoke with confidence, sitting up in the bed, her shoulders square and her chin tilted upwards to meet Fannie's gaze, and yet, it seemed to Fannie like this way of getting Jeb's attention would only embarrass Waneta and bring her pain. "Did you talk to mamm about this?" Fannie asked.

"She's the one who told me to do it. How do you think she won daed?"

The back of Fannie's throat was dry. "That's what mamm said?"

"You can ask her yourself tonight, when you're sleeping."

"What do you mean, sleeping? Isn't mamm at the hospital?"

"You're just going to have to trust me, okay? You do trust me, don't you?"

Slowly, Fannie nodded. Of course, she trusted her sister. How could she not? In many ways, Waneta had been like her mamm. She was five years older and had always taken charge of the household. "How did mamm sound, when you talked to her?" Fannie asked. "Better?"

"Much," Waneta said.

"We'll have to be home when the kinner get back from school, if we're going to Sarah's tomorrow."

"Oh, we'll be back well before then. Sarah already invited us to visit," Waneta said blithely. "And we've been cooped up in this house for too long."

Fannie remembered no such invitation, but she didn't want to argue with her sister, not when things were so close to returning to normal. "As long as we're back before four when the kinner return," Fannie said.

"Of course," Waneta said.

CHAPTER 13

The meeting with the school board went well, thankfully, but anticipation of Jeb's visit kept Sarah tossing and turning through the following night. When her mamm came to wake her, it seemed as though she'd spent her dreams running in place. She woke, eyelids heavy and heart beating a touch too fast. Sarah applied her nervous energy with relish to the housework: kneading three bags of Friendship Bread to bake on the morrow, cleaning the kitchen, and helping her mamm in the garden. When the welcome silhouette of a buggy came up the driveway, Sarah was with her mamm on the porch, mending small tears in her brothers' trousers.

"That must be Jebediah!" Sarah exclaimed, her face blossoming in a smile.

Sarah's mamm cocked her head. "He's a bit early," she said. "I thought he'd said 11:30."

"He said 11:30?" Sarah said, a bit annoyed that her mamm hadn't mentioned that piece of information.

Sarah's mamm stood. Sarah followed, her heart sinking as the buggy came closer. A tall, gangly woman sat in the driver's seat.

From her hunched posture, Sarah realized it must be Fannie. Beside her sat Waneta. The older girl waved, revealing a strip of white bandage across her palm. "Sarah!"

"What's she doing here?" Sarah muttered, not feeling at all charitable. "Shouldn't she be at home?"

"Sarah," her mamm said, giving Sarah's forearm a squeeze. "The Ordnung commands we be hospitable to our neighbors and receive them with a welcoming heart. As it says in Peter, *And above all things have fervent charity among yourselves: for charity shall cover the multitude of sins. Use hospitality one to another without grudging. As every man hath received the gift, even so minister the same one to another, as good stewards of the manifold grace of God.*"

Fannie pulled her buggy alongside Sarah's family buggy and gently brought the horse to a stop.

Fannie reached up and took Waneta's hand, helping her down.

Sarah said, "Did anyone at your quilting circle say anything about Waneta and Fannie visiting?"

"Nee," Sarah's mamm said. "But they are neighbors, and I can't imagine they aren't here without cause." Raising her voice, she waved Waneta and Fannie over with a cheerful Good Morning. "Guder Mariye!"

Fannie looked frankly relieved at the invitation. Sarah couldn't help but feel sympathy for the girl. When they'd climbed the steps to the porch, Sarah's mamm said, "What brings you by?"

Fannie looked at Waneta, who said, "Oh, Sarah told me at church that we could stop by this week, and today's weather is fair. My sister Fannie cooked, and we've brought food to share for luncheon, if it's not a bother…" her voice trailed off.

"Of course, you can join us," Sarah's mamm said. "When Sarah said you'd hurt yourself, I'd been planning to visit your home later on this week anyhow just to check and see how you were doing. You look quite well."

"It hurts a bit," Waneta said. "And I have to keep it dry and be careful with what kinds of things I do." Glancing at the pile of mending on the table between Sarah and her mamm's chairs, she said, "No sewing for the next week, but at least it's not my writing hand."

"That's good," Sarah's mamm agreed. "Why don't you two sit out here with Sarah, Waneta, and I'll go inside and get you kinner something to drink. We have iced tea and apple juice."

"Iced tea, please," Waneta said before anyone else could make a request.

"I'm fine with either," Sarah said, rising to help. The last thing she wanted was to make small talk with Waneta, but Fannie waved for Sarah to sit down. "I can help," she said in a soft voice and followed Sarah's mamm into the kitchen.

Waneta took the empty chair and beckoned for Sarah to sit. "Danki. For letting us stay for lunch," she said crossing her legs at the ankle. "I was fine, but Fannie's been getting a bit stir crazy, especially with having to do more than her share of the chores what with these stupid stitches." Waneta flipped her palm up and held the bandaged hand out with all of the gravitas of a church offering.

Waneta's expression was open and sincere, but Sarah had doubts. Fannie seemed far too embarrassed about this visit to have suggested it. In fact, the only one who seemed happy about the situation was Waneta, who continued talking with breezy confidence, "It's sweet of your mamm to offer to call on us."

"My mamm is a very kind woman," Sarah said. They sat in silence for a moment, staring out at the flies humming around the railing posts as the sun shed golden light on the fields beyond.

"You seem quiet," Waneta said. "Is everything okay?"

"I'm fine," Sarah said. Was it possible for Waneta to have somehow found out that Jeb intended to call on her this day, and thus made arrangements to insert herself in the middle of the visit? Sarah wanted to doubt herself for being so suspicious, but she couldn't help thinking back to Waneta's throwing herself into

Jeb's arms the night the horse spooked. She'd been far more concerned with his attention to her wound than the injury itself. Sarah asked, "What if we'd been out?"

"Excuse me?"

"It's generally polite to give some warning before you call on someone," Sarah said. "What if we hadn't been here for some reason?"

"Then I suppose Fannie and I would have had a picnic lunch." Waneta said. "If you really want us to leave, we can go."

"I didn't say—"

The front door opened, and Sarah's mamm came out, holding two glasses. Behind her stood Fannie, two more drinks in hand. Ice clinked against the side of the glass as Sarah's mamm held out an iced-tea. "Are you two doing okay?"

"Fine," Sarah said, before Waneta could start complaining again. Sarah's mamm was clearly sympathetic to Waneta, and Sarah knew she should have been as well, but she couldn't shake her doubts as to the other girl's motivations. Sarah stood, "Mamm, you should sit."

Sarah's mamm laughed. "I'm not so old yet that I can't stand for a few minutes while you two girls talk. We should bring some of the dining room chairs out as we're having guests. Fannie, didn't you say you'd brought food. Is it still in your buggy?"

"I'll get it," Fannie said. "If you don't mind, I'd like to get a bucket of water for our horse." Fannie said.

"Oh, I'll get John to take him to the pasture if you two are staying for lunch," Sarah's mamm said. "You just see to getting that food to the refrigerator."

"Yes, ma'am," Fannie said and started briskly down the stairs.

"Sarah, why don't you help me with these chairs," her mamm said. "Waneta, you just stay there and drink you tea. We can't have you causing more harm with that hand."

Sarah stood. As much as she didn't like the idea of leaving Waneta to her own devices on the porch, she was grateful for an excuse not to have to exchange small talk with the other girl. She followed her mamm into the dining room, the skylights and wide windows with fluttering yellow and green curtains giving the house a light, airy feel.

Sarah's mamm stopped in front of the table, and in a very low voice, almost a whisper asked, "What were you and Waneta talking about that had you so upset?"

"Nothing important," Sarah said.

"I know you're excited to see your young man, but that's no excuse to be rude."

"I wasn't rude," Sarah said. "If anyone is being rude, it's Waneta. She should have let us know somehow that she'd be visiting. I just asked what she'd have done if we were out."

"Those two girls are lonely, that much is obvious. Poor Fannie shies away at the slightest thing. It's no shame she got her daed's height, but growing so early has to be tough on the girl, even without her mamm's illness."

"I don't blame Fannie for anything," Sarah said, truthfully. "It just seems awfully convenient, that's all."

"What do you mean, convenient?"

"Waneta wants to court with Jebediah, that's what Annie told me." Hearing her own suspicions out loud, Sarah realized how petty she must sound. There was no conspiracy. There couldn't be one. How could Waneta even have known that Jebediah was going to call on Sarah at her home, on this day? "I know it sounds silly," she added, her cheeks warming.

"You've always been a sensible girl, but young men make fools of us all," Sarah's mamm said. "It's fortunate we do the same for them. Otherwise, it would be unfair indeed."

"I know there's no way Waneta could have known about today," Sarah said. "I just…"

"Well, better to get it in the open rather than have bad thoughts fester," Sarah's mamm said, picking up one of the chairs. "You take this one outside, and don't worry. I'll keep our guests entertained when young Jebediah calls, should the need be."

The sound of footsteps echoed down the hall. "Mrs. Lambright?" Fannie said, carrying a bowl covered in tinfoil. "This is a potato salad. It's my mamm's recipe. And I've got a bag full of bread as well from yesterday's baking. I'm really sorry to impose."

"It's no imposition, Fannie," Sarah's mamm said. "Why don't you give me this and take up another one of those chairs with Sarah to go on the porch. We're going to have some more company for lunch, so I'd best get started getting things together."

Fannie nodded and handed over the bowl. "Which of these chairs would be best?" she asked Sarah as her mamm made brisk pace towards the kitchen.

"Any one will do," Sarah said.

Fannie opened her mouth as though she wanted to say something else, then glancing down the hallway towards the porch, gave a minute shake of her head.

"Are you all right, Fannie?" Sarah asked.

"I'm sorry," Fannie lowered her gaze and lifted the chair closest to her from under the dining room table. "We shouldn't leave Waneta by herself for too long," she said.

"Fannie?"

"I'm fine," Fannie said.

"You didn't ask who was joining us for lunch." Sarah said.

Fannie shifted the chair in her arms. "I didn't want to be rude," she said, shrinking into herself even further. The poor girl has it hard enough, Sarah thought to herself. I shouldn't be interrogating her.

"Let's go have some of that tea," Sarah said.

"Danki," Fannie said, breathing a quiet sigh through her nose.

Just as they stepped onto the porch, a second buggy turned from the road and up their driveway. Jebediah! Sarah's heart leapt with joy.

When the buggy was close enough to see Jeb sitting straight-backed and handsome beneath his summer straw hat, Waneta stood and waved. "Jeb!" she shouted.

It could only have been bad timing that brought Waneta to their home at this very moment, still Sarah felt vaguely cheated as she waved to the advancing buggy, her movement an echo of Waneta's enthusiasm.

Between the two older girls, Fannie hunched over her chair, a reed bent in the face of the oncoming storm.

CHAPTER 14

Knowing that he was going to be seeing Sarah at her home this afternoon, Jebediah had taken special care to keep his clothing neat before riding over to Sarah's. It had been worth enduring the teasing of his younger brother for taking a bath in the middle of a workday, and shaving twice, but he wanted to look his best.

The sun was bright overhead, the sharp blue of the sky relieved only by cirrus clouds feathering high above. Jeb was grateful that Sarah lived close to his parent's house, less than fifteen minutes away by buggy. Normally, the gentle rattle of the buggy and steady plodding of Star's hooves over the asphalt road would have made for a pleasant journey, but anticipation of seeing Sarah made Jeb wish for a moment that he was behind the wheel of a fast moving Englischer car.

What kind of Amish man are you? Jeb chided himself as he caught sight of the break in the road that lead to Sarah's family farm. He guided Star to make the turn, glad that her usual placid temperament seemed to have returned. He'd debated taking Ebony, the other mare, but she'd been a bit off of her feed for the past few days, and Jeb's daed hadn't wanted to stress her before the veterinarian checked her over tomorrow afternoon.

As Jeb drove up to Sarah's house, he was surprised to see a second buggy and the silhouettes of three women on the porch. He'd only thought Sarah had younger brothers, who at this time ought to have been in school.

One of the women stood and waving at him yelled out his name. Jeb immediately recognized the voice. What was Waneta doing here? Of all of the rotten timing…

Jeb schooled his features into a smile and waved back. Now that he'd gotten closer to the house, he could see Sarah, standing closer to the porch waving, as well. Between the two young women stood Fannie, clutching the back of what looked like a dining room chair.

Jebediah slowed his horse just as Sarah's mamm and daed walked together from behind the house. Sarah's daed was pink from the sun, a sheen of sweat glistening on his skin. He nodded to Jebediah. Waneta's horse hadn't yet been unhooked from her buggy, and Sarah's mamm pointed at the two buggies, saying something to her husband who moved towards Jebediah with a purposeful stride. Jebediah parked his buggy a good distance from Waneta's, not knowing how the horses would react to each other, especially considering whatever had spooked Star the night before.

Sarah's mamm parted from her husband when they reached the driveway, walking back to the house and climbing the stairs onto the porch. After saying something to all three girls, they took up their chairs and began to file into the house.

"Mr. Lambright," Jebediah said when Sarah's daed was in speaking distance. "Sir, thank you for having me over. I was hoping there might be someplace I can put Star—"

"Ja, ja," Sarah's daed said. "We'll lead both to the pasture as it seems Waneta and Fannie will also be joining us for lunch." The man looked bemused. "My simple farm has become quite the gathering place it seems."

Jebediah ventured a smile. "If you want me to take a look at the chair you'd like to have me fix, I can do it after we tend to the horses."

Sarah's daed laughed. "In its own time, son," he said. That living room chair has been rocking for at least three years. We keep a folded up wad of newspaper under it, unattractive, but effective enough. I must admit, I'm impressed at your industriousness. Did Sarah tell you about the problem?"

"Actually, it was Annie who told Mark who told me."

"Well, as I said, I am impressed with you young people's care for the community. So you apprenticed in New York State?"

"Ja," Jeb said.

Sarah's daed asked him more about his work and life since

returning to Lancaster, questions all delivered in a mild tone that only a fool would believe revealed only mere curiosity. Jeb answered as thoroughly as he could, and Sarah's daed nodded, his lips twitching in the occasional genuine smile. When they'd finished with the horses, he clapped Jebediah once on the shoulder and said, "My children are my treasures. I do everything in my power to make certain they have as good a life under God's gentle hand as I am capable. There's nothing in my life that matters more to me."

"I understand, sir," Jebediah said. "I promise I'll..." What could he promise? Technically, he couldn't even tell Sarah's father that he was courting with her. At the same time, it was obvious all parties had seen through his relatively thin ruse with the chair.

Sarah's daed's face broke out in a large grin. "Gutt! Now why don't we take a look at that chair, while the women are preparing lunch?

After looking over the chair, which required very minor repairs at best, Sarah's mamm called them all into the dining room for lunch. It was a hearty lunch, chicken sandwiches on thick, home baked bread, potato salad, pickles and a pitcher of both iced tea and iced-coffee atop a bright, light green tablecloth. The men and women sat at opposite ends of the table, Sarah's daed and Jebediah across from the others. After bowing over his food in a silent grace, Jebediah ate heartily, and for a short time only the sound of chewing and the dull scrape of their forks over the plates was the only discernable sound.

Waneta held her fork awkwardly as she ate, wincing when it slipped through her fingers and clattered onto the plate.

"Did you bring your pain pills," Fannie asked at the same time Sarah's mamm asked, "Are you okay?"

"I'm fine," Waneta said. "The stitches only pull when I try to grip things."

"You must have been so frightened when the horse started to bolt," Sarah's mamm said, running her finger over the edge of her fork handle. "Did you ever find out what spooked her?"

"Not yet," Jebediah said. "Usually Star is as placid as a pond. She barely flicks her ears even when a big truck goes by, not that we get so many of those on the back roads. And she's been calm today."

"You brought her back out?" Sarah's mamm gave a disapproving head shake.

"Our other horse may have taken ill," Jeb said. "We have the veterinarian coming by tomorrow to look her over. And I checked Star thoroughly both last night and this morning. She's fine."

"I'm sure it wasn't her fault," Waneta chimed in. "Sometimes even the calmest horse will spook. It can be a shadow even, and you'll never know."

"Waneta knows a lot about horses," Fannie said. "She always tends our horses' hooves and talks to the farrier, especially with daed being so busy."

"It sounds like a lot of work," Jeb said.

"Waneta's always been a hard worker," Fannie said.

"Fannie," Waneta said. "You're embarrassing me." But the girl looked far from embarrassed, even as she averted her gaze to her food, her lips twitched upwards at the corners.

"I'm sorry," Fannie said and quietly started eating again.

Fannie was certainly a sensitive soul, Jeb thought as he took another bite of the potato salad. After swallowing, he said, "This is delicious, Mrs. Lambright."

"Oh, Waneta and Fannie brought it," Sarah's mamm said. "They said it's their mamm's recipe."

"I'm so glad you like it," Waneta said, holding her fork with no obvious discomfort. "It can be difficult to get the seasoning right. My mamm uses her own special recipe."

They finished with a hot apple pie from the oven, and then after returning their bowls to the kitchen, Jebediah said, "It's been my pleasure to have lunch with you. I'd like to come by at when I have the materials and finish working on that chair, if it's okay with you."

"Of course," Sarah's daed said.

"When do you think you'll be stopping by?" Waneta asked.

Jebediah was frankly floored by the directness of the question. It certainly wasn't Waneta's business when Jeb would return. Waneta's expression seemed mild enough, but Fannie had shrunk more in on herself, taking a small step backwards as though willing herself through sheer physical distance into the background.

"I'm not sure yet," Jebediah said. "It depends on how long it takes for me to get all of the materials." It was technically true, though Jebediah had little doubt he could acquire the few simple tools he needed in less than a week.

"Don't trouble yourself, young man," Sarah's daed said. "How about we see these two young women's horse, and then we can discuss the specifics at a later time. I'm assuming you'll need to be home before your brothers and sisters are off of school?"

"Ja," Fannie said before Waneta could open her mouth. "We need to get home. We're really grateful you had us over for lunch."

"Of course, Fannie," Mrs. Lambright took the girl's right hand and cupped it gently. "If there's anything you need, don't hesitate to ask."

Fannie looked down at the older woman, her eyes glistening in the sunlight streaming through the hallway skylight above. "Danki."

Jebediah walked back with Sarah's daed towards the pasture. When they'd gotten a good distance away, Mr. Lambright said, "I'm going to have to pray on some things. But we'll see those two young ladies on their way before we discuss any further business between us, if that's okay with you."

"Ja," Jeb said, trying to put all of his heartfelt gratitude into that simple syllable. Waneta clearly had more than friendly interest in him. As much as Jeb didn't want to believe it, his gut told him that Waneta had somehow been responsible for spooking Star, two nights and what felt like a lifetime ago. They'd all been distracted at first by Fannie's hysterics. Had the younger girl cried like that deliberately? Jebediah was inclined to doubt it. Fannie seemed genuinely distressed. Waneta however…

Jeb didn't know, but he was grateful, at least, that Sarah's daed were inclined to help. Once Waneta realized that Jeb and Sarah were courting, there'd be no reason for her to keep trying to capture Jeb's attention. No sane person would.

CHAPTER 15

They'd made it down the driveway and about five minutes down the road when Waneta said, "We left mamm's bowl at the Lambrights'."

"No, we didn't," Fannie said. "I put it in the buggy before we left. I remember."

"And I took it out. It's on their living room table. And now we're going to go back and get it."

Fannie's grip tightened on the reins. "Why would you do that?" Fannie asked. The calm of her tone belied a growing nervousness inside of her. All she wanted to do was go home and scrub something until she could see her reflection, clean and sweet smelling, inside of it.

"Because I want to see what Sarah and Jeb are up to," Waneta said.

"Jeb is going home, like us," Fannie said. "He got our horse first."

"He did get our horse first, but he didn't say he was going immediately home. What if they're together...now?"

"Then he's courting with her, and her parents approve," Fannie said. "I don't know why you're so determined to be with someone who doesn't love you."

Fannie wasn't even sure Jebediah liked Waneta. These days, Fannie had a difficult time liking Waneta herself. The acidity of her moods reminded Fannie of how mamm would sometimes get , spewing hate until her words slurred into tears, and she'd wind up rocking in the bed whimpering at them all to be quiet, though nobody had made a sound, not even daring to move or breathe lest it set off another storm.

"Turn Herb around," Waneta ordered.

Fannie kept her grip tight on the reins but didn't guide the horse from his path. "We can get the bowl back at Church the Sunday after next. It's fine."

"I don't give a—I don't care about the stupid bowl! Weren't you listening to me?"

"We're not going back."

"I said give me those reins!" Waneta grabbed at the

reins, but Fannie jerked them away. Startled, Herb shifted sharply to the left, dragging the buggy off of the shoulder and into the road.

"Stop it!" Fannie shouted. The buggy was rocking back and forth as their agitated horse began to trot diagonally towards the opposite lane. "We're going to get hurt!"

"Then *give me the reins*," Waneta spoke in sharp syllables, each word as heavy as an axe blow.

Fannie did her best to steady the horse, but Waneta grabbed at her hands, scratching deep into Fannie's skin. Fannie screamed and pulled back. The horse, now thoroughly confused, turned in the opposite direction from where he had been running, back into the middle of the road again.

Behind them, a car honked its horn. Normally, Herb was used to such noise and would simply move along, at most flicking an ear towards the obnoxious sound, but now he was agitated and stopped completely, his ears flat against his head.

"See what you've done?" Fannie said. "I'm going to go calm him down."

"I'm sorry," Waneta said, her voice losing that edge of acidic anger that had been so worrying before. Relieved, Fannie gave her a quick grin. "You just stay here. You really should be taking that pain pill. It hurts a lot, doesn't it?"

Waneta shrugged.

The car made a wide circle around the two of them, riding almost up onto the shoulder before continuing back onto the narrow, two-lane road. Fannie climbed down from the buggy and walked beside Herb, speaking in gentle, slow tones.

In the distance, Fannie saw the dark outline of a truck. She placed her hand on the horse's neck and focused on staying calm. It would do no good to show agitation herself, and the truck could see them and slow down if necessary. Then the reins jerked back. Herb whinnied and started to trot again.

"Waneta!" Fannie shouted, jumping out of the way of the buggy before it hit her. "What are you doing?"

Waneta said nothing and instead focused her gaze on the reins. Herb was running down the center of the road. The truck's horn blared, slowing as its driver slammed on the brakes.

Fannie ran after the buggy, which was now turning around in a wide arc as Waneta directed it back the way they'd come. Recognizing what Waneta was doing, Fannie tried to get ahead of the buggy. "Stop!" she shouted, but Waneta wasn't listening. "You can't just leave me here!"

"Then get back in," Waneta said.

A rough voice shouted from behind them, "What are you girls doing? Is everything okay?"

Fannie looked back at the truck, now arrived at a rumbling stop behind them. The driver had his window rolled down and leaned his head and shoulder out of it. He was a large man with a wide, flat nose, full cheeks and a gray smudge of a beard over his jaw.

"I'm sorry, sir," Fannie said. "My sister isn't feeling well."

"Well, it seems to have slowed down now, but one of you has to keep control of that horse," the driver said. "It's not safe."

"I know," Fannie said. "We're very sorry."

"Are you coming?" Waneta shouted from the buggy. Herb had stopped, but he was still agitated, his ears twitching at every noise as his body radiated tension. Waneta waved Fannie towards the buggy with her good hand. Not wanting to cause more trouble, Fannie nodded and ran up to join her sister.

"I'm going to go around you two girls," the trucker said. "Will you be able to keep that horse still?"

"It's fine," Waneta said.

The truck maneuvered itself around the buggy, giving as wide a berth as the road allowed, before rumbling off into the distance.

Though Waneta held a firm grip on the reins, blood had seeped into the bandage around her wound.

"You're bleeding," Fannie said.

Waneta looked down at her hands, and her face paled. "I didn't notice."

"Let me drive," Fannie said.

"Only if we're going back. It'll be better to wash the wound anyway. The Lambrights are closer."

Defeated, Fannie agreed. Taking the reins, the dark brown leather now stained with her sister's blood, Fannie prayed.

Dear God, I am like David, filled with fear in the face of a monster I can't see and don't understand. And now, Lord, what wait I for? My hope is in thee. Give me strength.

CHAPTER 16

After saying her grateful goodbyes to Fannie and Waneta, Sarah watched as her daed helped Jeb hook his horse back up to his buggy.

"It was good to see you again, Jeb," Sarah ventured.

"Ja," Jeb said, resting a hand on the neck of his horse. "I heard that you're going to start teaching in the autumn."

"It's not decided yet," Sarah said, modestly. "But I met with the school board and I think they liked me. I've already spoken with the Bishop about taking my baptismal vows in the fall. It's a bit unusual for me to be hired before I've officially accepted our faith, but with Mrs. Troyer's situation and the fact that I'm the only candidate, currently, I'm hopeful that if it's God's will that I'll begin in September."

"Wunderbar!" Jeb exclaimed, perhaps with a bit more enthusiasm than the revelation warranted. Sarah realized that her daed had walked around the back of the buggy, and with Jeb's horse obscuring the view of the pair of them from her mamm, still mending trousers on the porch, the two youths were effectively alone.

Sarah took a step towards him. "Do you plan to take your vows in the fall as well?"

"If I can find a woman willing to put up with me as a husband," he said, eyes shining in the blessed sunlight. "There's a youth soccer game Friday afternoon. It would be my pleasure if you accompanied me there."

"I'd love to!" Sarah said with her hands clasped together in joy.

Jeb took a step towards her. Looking up into his earnest face, the luminous green of his gaze, Sarah wanted to kiss him. Not that she'd be so daring, not when either of her parents could interrupt them at any point.

"Hoy!" Sarah's daed shouted. He'd taken a couple of steps out into the driveway and looked down the hill towards the road. "What's wrong?"

Sarah and Jeb stepped out on the driveway to join him. A buggy approached, and Sarah immediately recognized it and the two young women driving as Fannie and Waneta.

"What are they doing back here?" Jeb muttered under his breath, sounding not at all charitable.

Sarah felt the same.

Fannie slowed the buggy, bringing it to a stop beside Jeb's.

"I'm so sorry," Fannie said. "Waneta wanted to come back for our bowl, and then there was a mixup, and I think she broke some of the stitches on her hand."

Fannie climbed down and then held out her hand for Waneta. "Come on, we'll have to take that off in the kitchen and make sure it's not too bad." Glancing back at Sarah's daed, she added, "If it wasn't for her hand, I'd have just had us keep going home. The kinner will be back in an hour and a half, about."

"It's fine," Sarah's daed said. "Come on down, Waneta. Is your hand bleeding? I'll have my Anna take a look at that. You need to be careful about using it."

"Yes, she does," Fannie sounded genuinely annoyed, which was so out of the ordinary for the girl that Sarah was surprised.

Waneta stepped down from the buggy. "Jebediah," she said. "I'm surprised you're still here."

"I was discussing some things with Sarah."

Waneta's eyes narrowed. "Oh, I see."

"I was hoping to get to know her better," Jeb said.

"You've known each other since you were children."

"And now I wish to know her as an adult. It really isn't your business, Waneta. You really should see to your hand. I doubt you want it infected." Jeb nodded at both girls. Fannie gripped the back of Waneta's arm. "Come on, let's go," she said. Her grip was tight enough that Waneta winced, but she did walk.

"I'd best be going," Jeb said. "Until Friday?"

"Friday," Sarah said with a smile.

Though Jeb hadn't said they were directly courting, it would have been rude to do so in plain hearing of her daed, he'd made it clear where his interests lay. Sarah watched as Jeb climbed into his buggy and after giving her a slow nod and smile, guided his horse and buggy back onto the driveway and towards the road. The words of James 1:17 came to Sarah's mind. *Every good gift and every perfect gift is from above, and cometh down from the Father of lights, with whom is no variableness, neither shadow of turning.* Sarah and Jebediah might decide ultimately that they did not suit each other, but for now, the future seemed as bright as the sun overhead, and Sarah's heart whispered a prayer of Thanksgiving.

CHAPTER 17

Thankfully, they didn't have to return to the hospital. Sarah's mamm found a second bandage in a first-aid kit behind her sink and rewrapped Waneta's hand. Waneta was silent on the ride back, and Fannie didn't feel like talking either. Jeb had been quite clear about his interest in Sarah. Waneta could hardly ignore that, and if she did…

Fannie wasn't going to make things worse by helping her older sister pursue a man who didn't want her. Hopefully, without encouragement, Waneta would turn her attention to someone else. Or something else, though Fannie couldn't imagine what Waneta would do if she didn't get married. She'd never had any interest in pursuing work outside of the house, though if mamm hadn't been ill for so long, it might have been different. Waneta was certainly talented with crafts. Fannie remembered her selling small trinkets to Englischers at the monthly outdoor market before their mamm had grown too unpredictable for such excursions.

They got home just ten minutes ahead of the younger brothers and sisters.

"I know you don't like the painkillers, but maybe you should just take one and lie down," Fannie suggested when they got the kinner settled. "Daed will be back in a few hours, and Rachel and I can handle dinner."

"Fine," Waneta said. "I need to talk to mamm."

"You can't go to the hospital now!' Fannie said. "And you shouldn't be walking to the Fisher's three miles on your own to use their phone either."

"It's fine," Waneta said. "I'm just going upstairs, like you said. It's like you're my older sister. Or mamm."

Sometimes Fannie felt exactly that way. In four months, her own Rumspringa would begin, and already she felt like she'd lived a hundred years. One thing she had learned from this adventure with her older sister, she was never going to fall in love. Never court and never marry. It was too much trouble.

Waneta took a step towards the stairs, then stopped. "I'm sorry about all of this." She looked for a moment like she was about to cry. "I should have known nothing would come of it. I'm not a person who good things happen for."

"Don't say that!" Fannie took her sister's hands, forgetting her earlier annoyance. "Just because Jeb doesn't like you doesn't mean anything. It just means God has someone better for you!"

"I'm just like mamm," Waneta said. "I've tried to pretend I'm not, but…it's probably a good thing this didn't work out."

"Jeb's not good enough for you," Fannie said.

"I don't care about Jeb. I don't think I really did," Waneta said. "You'll be okay with daed and the kinner?"

"Ja, of course."

Instead of turning and going down the hallway towards the stairs, Waneta stared at Fannie. "None of this is your fault. I need you to know that."

"Waneta, what's wrong?"

"I'm sorry. I'm just tired." Waneta closed the distance between them and wrapped her arms around Fannie's waist. "I can't believe you've gotten so tall. It really is like you're the oldest."

"I'm not though," Fannie said.

"I know."

Waneta went upstairs, and Fannie gratefully threw herself into the unfinished household tasks until her daed came home. Her younger brothers and sisters were more cheerful than usual after school when their daed was out of the house. The youngest even stopped sucking her thumb and when asked, talked a bit about playing tag with the older girls at school.

As the afternoon darkened into evening, Fannie's mood settled. She'd whipped up a dinner mostly of leftovers: chicken and noodle casserole, boiled string beans, bread and pickles. She was putting it onto the dining room table when her daed came home. These five weeks had worn years onto their daed's face. He'd always been thin and strong from factory work, but grief and worry had burned the flesh from his bones: rendering his face sharp angles of light and shadow and his body skin over whipcord muscle, hidden only by the loose fabric of his trousers and shirt.

"Fannie, there you are. Where's Waneta, in the kitchen?"

"Nee. She had a problem with her hand," Fannie said, surprised her daed had even noticed Waneta was missing. Since his wife had been taken to the hospital, he hadn't noticed much. He'd only eat if food was put in front of him, speak when spoken to in short, nondescript sentences that illuminated little. At night, he'd spend hours sitting in front of his Bible, staring down at the words without turning a page while Waneta and Fannie cleaned up after dinner and saw to it that their younger brothers and sisters finished their homework, chores, and went to bed on time.

"Hand...oh yes, she injured it on Sunday," he said, with a vague wave. "How is she feeling?"

Fannie shrugged.

"Fannie?"

Upstairs, there was a heavy thump and then a clatter. "Waneta?" Fannie yelled up towards the stairs. She must have tried to lift something, though she should have known better with her injury. Hearing no answer, Fannie said, "I'll check on her."

Fannie climbed the stairs, feeling more winded than usual from the easy climb. Her heart beat a touch too fast and loud. "Waneta?" She knocked on the door of their shared room and got no response.

Fannie pushed the door open. The sun was almost set, painting the room in murky blue shadows. Their mamm's knitting was scattered across the floor between Waneta's bed and the dresser; the box that had held it leaned haphazardly against the wall, a deep crack through the base. Waneta sat on the bed, the open yellow bottle of hospital pain medication laying on its side on the quilt beside her. It took Fannie a horrified moment to realize the bottle was open and empty.

Waneta held her cupped palm to her lips. Fannie ran to her sister and yanked the older girl's hand away from her mouth. A rain of white tablets fell across the quilt.

"What are you doing!" Fannie screamed.

Waneta looked up at her and said, "I'm going to talk to mamm. She always visits me when I'm sleeping."

"Mamm's at the Philhaven hospital," Fannie said. Her hands were shaking, but sat herself down the bed, atop Waneta's pillow and started to gather up the fallen pills. How many had the hospital given Waneta?

"Did you take any of these before I got here?" Aside from the shaking, Fannie was calm. She'd endure this, even if the hospital had to come and take Waneta away as they'd done her mamm, Fannie would endure.

"It's fine. I'd have been fine."

"Did you take any?" The hospital had dispensed eight tablets. Fannie counted seven in her hand. "You only took one, is that right?"

Waneta nodded. "I just wanted to go to sleep."

Footsteps sounded from the hallway, and behind Fannie, the door creaked on its hinges. "Fannie?" It was their daed. "Waneta? The casserole was burning in the oven. I turned it off. What's going on? Why did you throw your knitting on the floor?"

Fannie turned her head to look at her daed. His gaze moved from her to the box of knitting on the floor. "This is your mamm's. What's it doing in here, and on the floor?"

"Waneta took it weeks ago," Fannie said. "Mamm kept it on her night table. You didn't even notice it was gone, did you?"

"I—"

"You don't pay attention to us," Fannie said. She was calm, but that calm seemed fragile now, a cap of ash over churning lava, like quiescent volcanoes that she'd learned about in school. "Waneta just tried to take all of her pain pills all at once. You should go downstairs and turn off the oven."

"Fannie..." her daed looked like he might cry.

The boiling fury that Fannie had been ignoring rose in spite of her best intentions. Fannie knew she should push this anger back down, seal it with rock and return to silence, but her heart seemed intent on spilling hateful, useless words and she couldn't stop herself. She didn't want to stop herself. "Why don't you take us to visit mamm? You hate her, don't you? You don't want her to come back. You just want us all to forget—"

"That's not true!"

"Then why? It's been almost six weeks. Doesn't she want to see us?" Fannie was crying now.

"It's not...she loves us...she loves all of us..."

"She's not there," Waneta said. "I hired a car and visited just before Jebediah came back. Daed won't tell me where she's been taken."

"I'm so sorry." Now her daed was crying. "God help me, I should never have kept it from you. I thought I was making it easier at first, and then I just couldn't...."

Fannie's mouth was dry. She hugged her arms around herself, the pills her sister had tried to take a hard lump in her palm. "Tell me what's going on. Tell me."

"You mamm, after she tried to take her own life, the doctors did what they could but she won't wake up. She may never wake up. They don't know."

"No." Fannie hugged herself tighter, bringing her knees up onto the bed.

"I didn't want to have you kinner see her like that. I thought it would be easier...but..."

"That's not true. Tell him Waneta! You said you'd seen her. You talked to her."

Waneta rocked forward, pulling at the roots of her hair with both hands. "I don't know," she repeated again and again until the words became indistinct sobs.

Their daed crossed the room and put his thin arms around both of his daughters. "I'm so sorry. It's all my fault. I should have taken her for help earlier. I should have kept a closer eye on her. On all of you. We'll visit your mamm tomorrow, and talk about things. No more lies. It's exactly as John says in the Bible. *Howbeit when he, the Spirit of truth, is come, he will guide you into all truth: for he shall not speak of himself; but whatsoever he shall hear, that shall he speak: and he will shew you things to come.* We can't live like this anymore, in the spirit of lies."

They clung to each other, and when Fannie's younger brothers and sister joined them, the revelations they shared were choked and painful, but when the storm passed, the quiet that followed was somehow lighter, and though her nose was stuffed, Fannie felt like for the first time since their mamm had been taken away, she could breathe.

CHAPTER 18

Though it was a sin to gossip, the shocking news that Waneta's daed had hidden his wife' suicide attempt and resultant coma from the community and even his own children was too much to ignore. Sarah heard bits and snatches of the talk, but she was far too busy with her own affairs busy to concern herself with even the low levels of idle gossip that blossomed between people, no matter their good intentions. The school board had accepted her to teach in the fall, and she spent all of the Wednesday after Waneta's surprise visit helping Mrs. Troyer in the schoolhouse. Then there was her growing relationship with Jebediah.

Three days after Waneta's visit to their home, Sarah's mamm announced at breakfast that they would be delivering two casseroles, four loaves of bread, and a smattering of household goods to the Bechler household that morning.

"Are you sure?" Sarah asked. She'd rather have avoided Waneta, considering the other young woman's obsession with Jebediah, but there was no arguing with her mamm so once the younger kinner were packed off to school, they loaded up the buggy and made a quick pace to the Bechler's.

The home and lands showed signs of disrepair: white paint peeling at the base of the farmhouse, unsightly weeds peeking up between the young tomato plants in the garden, and a downed fencepost around the tiny pasture that housed their horse, who stood munching idly at a patch of grass.

"We should have visited much sooner," Sarah's mamm said, looking over the house and lands as they rode up the driveway.

Though it was Friday and most Amish preferred to do their wash at the beginning of the week, Fannie stood at the back of her house, hanging sheets on the line. She looked up, visibly surprised as Sarah's mamm parked the buggy on the shoulder of the driveway beside the house.

Fannie dropped the sheet she'd just been hanging back into the basket and then waved at the two women. "Sarah! Mrs. Lambright! Is everything okay?"

"We're just being good neighbors," Sarah's mamm said. "Sarah, grab up those casseroles." Looking back at Fannie, she said, "We had some extra food, and we wanted to drop it by. How's your sister doing?"

Fannie's face went white. She blinked twice and looked down at her hands. "Fine. She's fine. Her hand I mean. She's with daed."

"He's not working today?"

"He took the rest of the week off. We needed the time. I suppose you heard about our mamm."

"A terrible thing," Sarah's mamm said. "It must be difficult for all of you."

"Ja."

"Well, help us bring in this food, Fannie. We'll cook up a nice lunch for you and your family."

They took in the food. Waneta was with her daed in the living room. They'd been talking, but both looked up as Sarah and her mamm the entrance, food in hand. On the sofa, Waneta looked thin and wrung out, but when she smiled at Sarah, the expression seemed more genuine, if weaker, than any of the enthusiastic gregariousness that she'd expressed in the weeks prior.

"Daed," Waneta said. "If you don't mind helping the Lambrights with their horse, I'd like to speak with Sarah for a minute. If it's not too much trouble."

"Of course, Waneta," her daed rested his palm on Sarah's hands, clasped in her lap.

Fannie took the casseroles and followed Sarah's mamm towards the kitchen, while Sarah stood in the middle of Waneta's living room, unsure what to do next.

"You can sit," Waneta said, gesturing towards the half of the sofa where her daed had left. "I guess you've heard about my mamm."

"Some," Sarah said. "I try not to pay attention to gossip."

Waneta's eyes narrowed, and she nodded. "You actually mean that. I'm sorry, it's just…with everything…"

"It's fine," Sarah said, awkwardly.

"No, it isn't. I owe you an apology. I shouldn't have interfered with your courtship with Jebediah. He never wanted me. I want to apologize," Waneta said. "I haven't treated you fairly, and you've been kind to me."

"It's in the past," Sarah said. "With everything that's been going on with you and your family…" Sarah nodded. A part of Sarah was still angry at Waneta, but in order to take her baptismal vows, Sarah would have to learn to forgive. She took the other girl's hands and cupped them inside of her own. "We can be friends now," she said. "If you still want that."

Waneta ducked her head, blinking rapidly. "Danki."

Sarah said, "So my little brother and your little sister will be in my class together next year."

Waneta nodded. "Ja. And don't let Rachel get away with burying her vegetables outside in the schoolyard when she doesn't want to eat them at lunch."

Sarah smiled. It was a bit forced, but as she and Waneta talked, their conversation grew easier, and Sarah found herself admiring the humor and strength of the other girl.

When Waneta's daed and Fannie returned to call Sarah and Waneta for lunch, the two girls sat, their heads close together and laughing as from the kitchen, the cinnamon smell of Sarah's mamm's special Friendship Bread filling the house with sweetness and love.

Peace I leave with you, my peace I give unto you: not as the world giveth, give I unto you. Let not your heart be troubled, neither let it be afraid.

–John 14:27

--

The End.

Thank you for reading Amish Friendship Bread – Book 1.

I hope you loved reading it as much as I loved writing it.

ABOUT THE AUTHOR

Ruth Price is a Pennsylvania native and devoted mother of four. After her youngest set off for college, she decided it was time to pursue her childhood dream to become a fiction writer. Drawing inspiration from her faith, her husband and love of her life Harold, and deep interest in Amish culture that stemmed from a childhood summer spent with her family on a Lancaster farm, Ruth began to pen the stories that had always jabbered away in her mind. Ruth believes that art at its best channels a higher good, and while she doesn't always reach that ideal, she hopes that her readers are entertained and inspired by her stories.

Made in the USA
Middletown, DE
06 April 2015